KING'S BLOOD FOUR

I stared down, impotent to move or call. Couldn't the King see who stood there? Demon and Tragamor, substance and shade, True Game challenged upon him, and the very air alive with cold. King's Blood Four, here, now.

I reached a hand, fumbled at the Prince's sleeve. "No, no, it's not courteous . . . not courteous . . ." My hand was slapped away by an armored glove, struck so violently that it lay bleeding upon the table before me.

The King called again. "Is it not forbidden to call challenge during Festival?"

"Many things are forbidden, Mertyn. Many things. Still, we do them."

"True. Well, if you would have it so, Prince—then have it so. I move."

And from behind one of the crystal fountains came that lonely Sorcerer I had wondered at, striding into the light until he stood just behind the King, full of silent waiting, clear as glass, holding the terrible thing he had been given to hold.

Other fantasy titles available from
Ace Science Fiction and Fantasy:

The Face in the Frost, *John Bellairs*
Peregrine: Primus, *Avram Davidson*
The Borribles, *Michael de Larrabeiti*
The Broken Citadel, *Joyce Ballou Gregorian*
Journey to Aprilioth, *Eileen Kernaghan*
900 Grandmothers, *R. A. Lafferty*
Swords and Deviltry, *Fritz Leiber*
The Seekers of Shar-Nuhn, *Ardath Mayhar*
The Door in the Hedge, *Robin McKinley*
Jirel of Joiry, *C. L. Moore*
Witch World, *Andre Norton*
Tomoe Gozen, *Jessica Amanda Salmonson*
The Warlock Unlocked, *Christopher Stasheff*
Bard, *Keith Taylor*
The Devil in a Forest, *Gene Wolfe*
Shadow Magic, *Patricia C. Wrede*
Changeling, *Roger Zelazny*

and much more!

KING'S BLOOD FOUR

SHERI S. TEPPER

ACE FANTASY BOOKS
NEW YORK

KING'S BLOOD FOUR

An Ace Fantasy Book/published by arrangement with the
author

PRINTING HISTORY
Ace edition/April 1983

ISBN: 0-441-44524-1

Ace Fantasy Books are published by Charter Communications, Inc.

200 Madison Avenue, New York, New York 10016
PRINTED IN THE UNITED STATES OF AMERICA

THE ORDER OF DESCENT BY LINEAGE

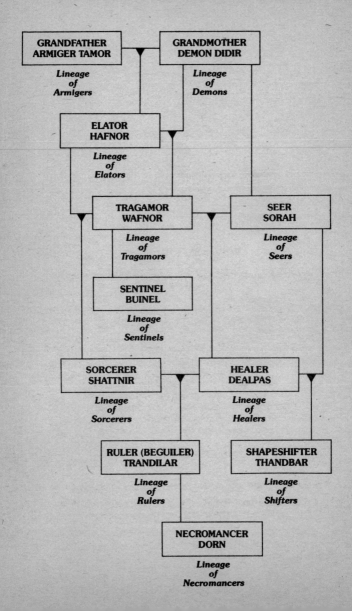

1

King's Blood Four

"Totem to King's Blood Four." The moment I said it, I knew it was wrong. I said, "No!"

Gamesmaster Gervaise tapped the stone floor with his iron-tipped staff, impatiently searching our faces for a lifted eye or for a raised hand. "No?" he echoed me. Of the three Gamesmasters of Mertyn's House, I liked Gervaise the best.

"When I said 'no,' I meant the answer wasn't quite right." Behind me Karl Pig-face gave a sneaky gasp as he always does when he is about to put me down, but Gamesmaster Gervaise didn't give him a chance.

"That's correct," he agreed. "Correct that it isn't quite right and might be very wrong. The move is one we haven't come across before, however, so take your time. Before you decide upon the move, always remember who you are." He turned away from us, staff tap-tapping across the tower room to the high window which gaped across the dark bulk of Havad's House down to River Reave where it wound like a tarnished ribbon among all the other School Houses—each as full of students as a dog is of fleas, as Brother Chance, the cook, would say. All the sloped land between the Houses was crowded full of dwellings and shops, all humping their way up the hills to the shuttered Festival Halls, then scattering out among the School Farms which extended

1

to the vacant land of the Edge. I searched over the Gamesmaster's shoulder for that far, thin line of blue which marked the boundaries of the True Game. Karl cleared his throat again, and I knew his mockery was only deferred, unless I could find an answer quickly. I wouldn't find it by staring out at Schooltown.

I turned back to the game model which hung in the air before us, swimming in icy haze. Somewhere within the model, among the game pieces which glowed in their own light or disappeared in their own shadow— somewhere in the model was the Demesne, the focal area, the place of power where a move could be of significance. On our side, the students' side, Demon loomed on a third level square casting a long, wing-shaped shadow. Two fanged Tragamors boxed the area to either side. Before them stood Gamesmaster Gervaise's only visible piece, the King, casting ruddy light before him. It was King's Blood Four, an Imperative— which meant I had to move something. None of the battle pieces were right; it had to be something similar to Totem. Almost anything could be hiding behind the King, and Gamesmasters don't give hints. Something similar, of like value, something . . . then I had it.

"Talisman," I blurted. "Talisman to King's Blood Four."

"Good." Gervaise actually smiled. "Now, tell me why!"

"Because our side can't see what pieces may be hiding behind the King. Because Talisman is an absorptive piece, that is, it will soak up the King's play. Totem is reflective. Totem would splash it around, we'd maybe lose some pieces . . ."

"Exactly. Now, students, visualize if you please. We have King, most durable of the adamants, whose 'blood,' that is, essence, is red light. Demon, most powerful of the ephemera, whose essence is shadow.

Tragamors making barriers at the sides of the Demesne. The player is a student, without power, so he plays Talisman, an absorptive piece of the lesser ephemera. Talisman is lost in play, 'sacrificed' as we say. The player gains nothing by this, but neither does he lose much, for with this play the Demesne is changed, and the game moves elsewhere in the purlieu."

"But, Master," Karl's voice oozed from the corner. "A strong player could have played Totem. A powerful player."

I flushed. Of course. Everyone in the room knew that, but students were not strong, not powerful, even though Karl liked to pretend he was. It was just one more of his little pricks and nibbles, like living with a hedgehog. Gamesmaster tilted his head, signifying he had heard, but he didn't reply. Instead, he peered at the chronometer on the wall, then out the window to check where the mountain shadow fell upon the harbor, finally back to our heavily bundled little group. "So. Enough for today. Go to the fires and your supper. Some of you are half frozen."

We were all half frozen. The models could only be controlled if they were kept ice cold, so we spent half our lives shivering in frigid aeries. I was as cold as any of them, but I wanted to let Karl get out of the way, so I went to the high window and leaned out to peer away south. There was a line of warty little islands there separating the placid harbor with its wheeling gulls from the wide, stormy lake and the interesting lands of the True Game beyond. I mumbled something. Gervaise demanded I repeat it.

"It's boring here in Schooltown," I repeated, shamefaced.

He didn't answer at once but looked through me in that very discomforting way the Masters sometimes have. Finally he asked me if I had not had Gamesmaster

Charnot for Cartography. I said I had.

"Then you know something of the lands of the True Game. You know of the Dragon's Fire purlieu to the North? Yes. Well, there are a King and Queen there who decided to rear their children Outside. They wanted to be near their babies, not send them off to a distant Schooltown to be bored by old Gamesmasters. They thought to let the children learn the rules of play by observation. Of the eight sons born to that Queen, seven have been lost in play. The eighth child sleeps this night in Havad's House nursery, sent to Schooltown at last.

"It is true that it is somewhat boring in Schooltown, and for no one more so than the Masters! But, it is also safe here, Peter. There is time to grow, and learn. If you desire no more than to be a carter or laborer or some other pawn, you may go Outside now and be one. However, after fifteen years in Mertyn's House, you know too much to be contented as a pawn, but you won't know enough for another ten years to be safe as anything else."

I remarked in my most adult voice that safety wasn't everything.

"That being the case," he said, "you'll be glad to help me dismantle the model."

I bit my tongue. It would have been unthinkable to refuse, though taking the models apart is far more dangerous than putting them together. Most of us have burn scars from doing one or the other. I sighed, concentrated, picked a minor piece out of the game box at random and named it, "Talisman!" as I moved it into the Demesne. It vanished in a flash of white fire. Gervaise moved a piece I couldn't see, then the King, which released the Demon. I got one Tragamor out, then got stuck. I could not remember the sequence of moves necessary to get the other Tragamor loose.

One thing about Gervaise. He doesn't rub it in. He just looked at me again, his expression saying that he knew what I knew. If I couldn't get a stupid Tragamor out of the model, I wouldn't survive very long in the True Game. Patiently, he showed me the order of moves and then swatted me, not too gently.

"It's only a few days until Festival, Peter. Now that you're fifteen, you'll find that Festivals do much to dispel boredom for boys. So might a little more study. Go to your supper."

I galloped down the clattering stairs, past the nurseries, hearing babies crying and the unending chatter of the baby-tenders; down past the dormitories, smelling wet wool and steam from the showers; into the fire-warm commons hall, thinking of what the Gamesmaster had said. It was true. Brother Chance said that only the powerful and the utterly unimportant lived long in the True Game. If you weren't the one and didn't want to be the other, it made sense to be a student. But it was still very dull.

At the junior tables the littlest boys were scaring each other with fairy tales about the lands of the Immutables where there was no True Game. Silly. If there weren't any True Game, what would people do? At the high table the senior students, those about to graduate into the Game, showed more decorum, eating quietly under the watchful eyes of Gamesmaster Mertyn, King Mertyn, and Gamesmaster Armiger Charnot. Most of those over twenty had already been named: Sentinel, Herald, Dragon, Tragamor, Pursuivant, Elator. The complete list of Gamesmen was said to be thousands of titles long, but we would not study Properties and Powers in depth until we were older.

At the visitor's table against the far wall a Sorcerer was leafing through a book as he dawdled over his food, the spiked band of his headdress glittering in the firelight. He was all alone, the only visitor, though I searched carefully for one other. My friend Yarrel was crowded in at the far end of a long table with no space near, so I took an open bench place near the door. Across from me was Karl, his red, wet face shining slickly in the steam of the food bowls.

"Y'most got boggled up there, Peter-priss. Better stick to paper games with the littly boys."

"Oh, shut up, sweat-face," I told him. It didn't do any good to be nice to Karl, or to be mean. It just didn't matter. He was always nasty, regardless. "You wouldn't have known either."

"Would so. Grandsire and Dadden both told me that 'un." His face split into his perpetual mocking grin, his point made. Karl was son of a Doyen, grandson of a Doyen, third generation in the School. I was a Festival Baby, born nine months after Festival, left on the doorsteps of Mertyn's House to be taken in and educated. I might as well have been hatched by a toad. Well, I had something Karl didn't. He could have his family name. I had something else.

Not that the Masters cared whether a student was first generation or tenth. There were more foundlings in the room than there were family boys. "Sentlings," those sent in from outside by their parents, had no more status than foundlings, but the family boys did tend to stick together. It took only a little whipping-on from someone like Karl to turn them into a hunting pack. Well, I refused to make a chase for them. Instead, I stared away down the long line of champing jaws and lax bodies. They all looked as I felt—hungry, exhausted from the day's cold, luxuriating in warmth, and grateful night had come. I thought of the promised Festival.

I would sew bells onto my trouser hems, stitch ribbons into the shoulder seams of my jacket, make a mask out of leather and gilt, and so clad run through the streets of

Schooltown with hundreds of others dressed just as I, jingling and laughing, dancing to drum and trumpet, eating whatever we wanted. During Festival, nothing would be forbidden, nothing required, no dull studies, the Festival Halls would be opened, people would come from Outside, from the School Houses, from everywhere. Bells would ring . . . and ring . . .

The ringing was the clangor of my bowl and spoon upon the stones where I had thrust them in my sleep. The room was empty except for one lean figure between me and the fire: Mandor, Gamesmaster of Havad's House, teeth gleaming in the fireglow.

"Well, Peter. Too tired to finish your supper?"

"I . . . I thought you weren't coming."

"Oh, I drift here and there. I've been watching you sleep for half an hour after bidding some beefy boy to leave you alone. What have you done to attract his enmity?"

I think I blushed. It wasn't anything I wanted to talk about. "Just . . . oh, nothing. He's one who always picks on someone. Usually someone smaller than he is, usually a foundling."

"Ah." He understood. "A Flugleman. You think?"

I grinned weakly. It would be a marvelous vengeance if Karl were named Flugleman, petty tyrant, minor piece, barely higher than a pawn. "Master Mandor, no one has yet named him that."

"You needn't call me Master, Peter."

"I know." Again, I was embarrassed. He should know some things, after all. "It's just easier than explaining."

"You feel you have to explain?"

"If someone heard me."

"No one will hear you. We are alone. Still, if this place is too public, we'll go to my room." And he was sweeping out the door toward the tunnel which led to

Havad's House before I could say anything. I followed him, of course, even though I had sworn over and over I would not, not again.

The next morning I received a summons to see King Mertyn. It didn't exactly surprise me, but it did shock me a little. I'd known someone was going to see me or overhear us, but each day that went by let me think maybe it wouldn't happen after all. I hadn't been doing anything different from what many of the boys do in the dormitories, nothing different from what I'd refused to do with Karl. Oh, true, it's forbidden, but lots of things are forbidden, and people do them all the time, almost casually.

So, I didn't know quite what to expect when I stood before the Gamesmaster in his cold aerie, hands in my sleeves, waiting for him to speak. I was shocked at how gentle he was.

"It is said you are spending much time with Gamesmaster Mandor of Havad's House. That you go to his room, spend your sleep time there. Is this true?" He was tactful, but still I blushed.

"Yes, Gamesmaster."

"You know this is forbidden."

"Gamesmaster, he bade me . . ."

"You know he is titled Prince and may bid as he chooses. But, it is still forbidden."

I got angry then, because it wasn't fair. "Yes. He may bid as he chooses. And I am expected to twist and tarry and try to escape him, like a pigeon flying from a hawk. I am expected to bear his displeasure, and he may bid as he chooses . . ."

"Ah. And have you indeed twisted and tarried and tried? Hidden among the books of the library, perhaps? Pled sanctuary from the head of your own House? Taken minor game vows before witnesses? Have you done these things?"

I hadn't. Of course I hadn't. How could I. Prince Mandor was my friend, but more than a friend. He cared about me. He talked to me about everything, things he said he couldn't tell anyone else. I knew everything about him; that he had not wanted to leave the True Game and teach in a Schooltown; that he hated Havad's House, that he wanted a House of his own; that he picked me as a friend because there was no one, no one in Havad's House he cared for. The silence between the Gamesmaster and me was becoming hostile, but I couldn't break it. At last he said, "I must be sure you understand, Peter. You must be aware of what you do, each choice you make which aids or prevents your mastery of the Game. You cannot stand remote from this task. You are in it. Do you know that?"

I nodded, said, "We all know that, Gamesmaster."

"But do you perceive the reality of it? How your identity will emerge as you play, as your style becomes unique, as your method becomes clear. Gradually it will become known to the Masters—and to you—what you are: Prince or Sorcerer, Armiger or Tragamor, Demon or Doyen, which of the endless list you are. You must be one of them, or else go down into Schooltown and apprentice yourself to a shopkeeper as some failed students do."

"It is said we are born to it," I objected, wanting to stop his talk which was making me feel guilty. "Karl says he will be Doyen because father and grandfather were Doyens before him. Born to it."

"What Karl may say or do or think is not important to you. What you are or may become should be important." He seized me by the shoulders and turned me to stare out the tall window. "Look there. In ten years you must go out there, ready or not, willing or not. In ten years you must leave this protected town, this Schooling place. In ten years you will join the True Game.

"You do not know this, but it was I who found you,

years ago, outside Mertyn's House, a Festival Baby, a soggy lump in your bright blankets, chewing your fist. If you have anyone to stand Father to you, it is I. It may be unimportant, but there is at least this tenuous connection between us which leads me to be concerned about you." He leaned forward to lay his face against mine, a shocking thing to do, as forbidden as anything I had ever done.

"Think, Peter. I cannot force you to be wise. Perhaps I will only frighten you, or offend you, but think. Do not put yourself in another's hands." Abruptly he left me there in the high room, still angry, confused, wordless.

"Do not put yourself in another's hands." The first rule of the game. Make alliances, yes, they told us, but do not give yourself away to become merely a pawn. This is why they forbid us so many things, deny us so much while we are young and defenseless. I leaned on the sill of the high window where golden sunlight lay in a puddle. A line of similar color reflected from a high House across the river, Dorcan's House, a woman's house. I wondered if they gamed there as we did; learning, waiting for their Mistresses and peers to name them, being bored. I knew little about women. We would not study the female pieces for some years yet, but the sight of that remote house made me wonder what names they had, what name I would have.

It was said among the boys that one could sometimes tell what name one would bear by the sound of it in one's own ears. I tried that, speaking into the silent air. "Armiger. Tragamor. Elator. Sentinel." Nothing. "Flugleman," I whispered, fearfully, but there was no interior response to that, either. I had not mentioned the name I dreamed of, the one I most desired to have, for I felt that to do so would breed ill luck. Instead, I called, "Who am I?" into the morning silence. The only reply came in a spate of gull-scream from the harbor,

like impersonal laughter. I told myself it didn't matter
who I was so long as I had more than a friend in Mandor.
A bell tolled briefly from the town, and I knew I had
missed breakfast and would be late for class.

In the room below, the windows were shut for once to
let the fire sizzling upon the hearth warm the room.
That meant no models that day, only lectures; dull,
warm words instead of icy, exciting movement.
Gamesmaster Gervaise was already stalking to and fro,
mumble-murmuring toward the cluster of student
heads, half of them already nodding in the unaccus-
tomed heat.

"Yesterday we evolved a King's game," he was saying. "Those of you who were paying attention would
have noticed the sudden emergence of the Demesne
from the purlieu. This sudden emergence is a frequent
mark of King's games. Kings do not signal their inten-
tions. There is no advance 'leakage' of purpose. There
may be a number of provocations or incursions without
any response, and then, suddenly, there will be an area
of significant force and intent—a Measurable Demesne.
Think how this differs from a battle game between Armigers, for instance, where the Demesne grows very
gradually from the first move of a Herald or Sentinel.
Just as the Demesne may emerge rapidly in a King's
game, so it may close as rapidly. Mark this rule, boys.
The greater the power of the piece, the more rapid the
consequence." He rattled his staff to wake the ones
dozing. "Note this, boys, please. If a powerful player
were playing against the King's side, the piece played
might have been one of the reflective durables such as
Totem, or even Herald. In that case . . ."

He began to drone again. He was talking about
measuring, and it bored everyone to death. We'd had
measuring since we came into class from the nurseries,

and if any of us didn't know how to measure a Demesne by now, it was hopeless. I looked for Yarrel. He wasn't there, but I did see the visiting Sorcerer leaning against the back wall, his lips curved in an enigmatic smile. "Sorcerer," I defined to myself, automatically. "Quiet glass, evoking but unchanged by the evocation, a conduit through which power may be channeled, a vessel into which one may pour acid, wine, or fire and from which one may pour acid, wine, or fire." I shivered. Sorcerers were very major pieces indeed, holders of the power of others, and I'd never seen or heard of one going about alone. It was very strange to have one leaning against the classroom wall, all by himself, and it gave me an itchy, curious feeling. I decided to sneak down to the kitchen and ask Brother Chance about it. He had been my best source of certain kinds of information ever since I was four and found out where he hid the cookies.

"Oh, my, yes," he agreed, sweating in the heat of the cookfire as he gave bits of meat to the spit dog. He poked away at the Masters' roast with a long fork. The odors were tantalizing. My mouth dropped open like a baby bird's, and he popped a piece of the roast into it as though I had been another spit dog. "Yes, odd to have a Sorcerer wandering about loose, as one might say. Still, since King Mertyn returned from Outside to become Gamesmaster here, he has built a great reputation for Mertyn's House. A Sorcerer might be drawn here, seeking to attach himself. Or, there are always those who seek to challenge a great reputation. It probably means no more than the fact that Festival is nigh-by, only days away, and the town is full of visitors. Even Sorcerers go about for amusement, I suppose. What is it to you, after all?"

"No one ever tells us anything," I complained. "We never know what's going on."

"And why should you? Arrogant boy! What is it to

you what Sorcerers do and don't do?" Ask too many questions and be played for a pawn, I always say. Keep yourself to yourself until you know what you are, that's my advice to you, Peter. But then, you were always into things you shouldn't have bothered with. Before you could talk, you could ask questions.

"Well, ask no more now. You'll get yourself into real trouble. Here. Take this nice bit of roast and some hot bread to sop up the juices and go hide in the garden while you eat it. It's forbidden, you know."

Of course I knew.

Everything was forbidden.

Roast was forbidden to boys. As was sneaking down to the kitchens.

As was challenging True Game in a Schooltown. Or during Festival.

As was this, and that, and the other thing. Then, come Festival, nothing would be forbidden. In Festival, Kings could be Jongleurs, Sentinels could be Fools, men could be women and women men for all that. And Sorcerers could be . . . whatever they liked. It was still confusing and unsettling, but the lovely meat juices running down my throat did much to assuage the itchy feeling of curiosity, guilt, and anger.

Late at night I lay in the moonlight with my hand curled on Mandor's chest. It threw a leaflike shadow there which breathed as he breathed, slowly elongating as the moon fell. "There is a Sorcerer wandering about," I murmured. "No one knows why." Under my hand his body stiffened.

"With someone? Talking with anyone?"

I murmured sleepily, no, all alone.

"Eating with anyone? At table with anyone?"

I said, no, reading, eating by himself, just wandering about. Mandor's graceful body relaxed.

"Probably here for the Festival," he said. "The town is filling up, with more swarming in every day . . ."

"But, I thought Sorcerers were always with someone."

He laughed, lips tickling my ear. "In theory, lovely boy, in theory. Actually, Sorcerers are much like me and you and the kitchen churl. They eat and drink and delight in fireworks and travel about to meet friends. He may be meeting old friends here."

"Maybe." My thought trailed off into sleepy drifting. There had been something a little feverish about Mandor's questions, but it did not seem to matter. I could see the moonlight reflected from his silver, serpent's eyes, alert and questing in the dark. In the morning I remembered that alertness with some conjecture, but lessons drove it out of my head. A day or two later he sought me out to give me a gift.

"I've been looking for you, boy, to give you something." He laughed at my expression, teasingly. "Go on. Open it. I may give you a gift for your first Festival. It isn't forbidden! It isn't even discouraged. Open it."

The box was full of ribbons, ribbons like evening sky licked with sunset, violet and scarlet, as brilliant and out of place in the gray corridor as a lily blooming in a crypt. I mumbled something about already having bought my ribbons.

"Poof," he said. "I know what ribbons boys buy. Strips of old gowns, bought off rag pickers. No. Take these and wear them for me. I remember my first Festival, when I turned fifteen. It pleases me to give them to you, my friend . . ."

His voice was a caress, his hands gentle on my face, and his eyes spoke only affectionate joy. I leaned my head forward into those hands. Of course I would wear them. What else could I do? That afternoon I went to beg needle and thread from Brother Chance. Gamesmaster Mertyn was in the kitchen, leaning against a cupboard, licking batter like a boy. I turned to go, but he beckoned me in and made me explain my business there, insisting upon seeing the ribbons when I had mumbled some explanation.

"Fabulous," he said in a tight voice. "I have not seen their like. Well, they do you credit, Peter, and you should wear them in joy. Let me make you a small gift as well. Strip out of your jacket, and I'll have my servant, Nitch, sew them into the seams for you." So I was left shivering in the kitchen, clad from the waist up only in my linen. I would rather have sewn them myself, even if King Mertyn's manservant would make a better job of it, and I said as much to Chance.

"Well, lad. The high and powerful do not always ask us what we would prefer. Isn't that so? Follow my rule and be in-conspic-u-ous. That's best. Least noticed is least bothered, or so I've always thought. Best race up to the dormitory and get into your tunic, boy, before you freeze."

Which I did, and met Yarrel there, and we two went onto the parapet to watch the Festival crowds flowing into town. The great shutters had been taken from the Festival Halls; pennants were beginning to flicker in the wind; the wooden bridge rolled like a great drum under the horses' hooves. We saw one trio go by with much bravura, a tall man in the center in Demon's helm with two fanged Tragamors at his sides. Yarrel said, "See there. Those three come from Bannerwell where your particular friend, Mandor, comes from. I can tell by the horses." Yarrel was a sentling, a farrier's son who cared more for horses than he ever would for the Game. He cared a good deal for me, too, but was not above teasing me about my particular friend. Well, I thought Yarrel would not stay in the School for ten years more. He would go seek his family and the countryside, all for the sake of horses.

I asked him how he knew that Mandor had come from

Bannerwell, but he could not remember. He had heard
it somewhere, he supposed.

Nitch brought the jacket that evening, sniffing a little
to show his disapproval of boys in general. It felt oddly
stiff when I took it, and my inquiring look made Nitch
sniff the louder. "There was nothing left of the lining,
student. It was all fallen away to lint and shreds, so while
I had the seams open, I put in a bit of new wadding.
Don't thank me. My own sense of the honor of Mertyn's
House would have allowed no less." And he sniffed
himself away, having spoken directly to me for the first
and last time.

I was glad of the new lining come morning, for we put
on our Festival garb and masks while it was still cold.
Yarrel smoothed the ribbons for me, saying they made a
lovely fall of color. We had sewn on our bells and made
our masks, and as soon as it was full light we were away,
our feet pounding new thunder out of the old bridge.
Yarrel's ribbons were all green, so I could pick him from
the crowd. All the tower boys wore ribbons and bells
which said, "Student here, student here, hold him
harmless for he is yet young . . ." Thus we could thieve
and trick during the time of Festival without hindrance,
though it were best, said the Masters, to do it in
moderation.

And we did. We were immoderately moderate. We
ate pork pies stolen from stalls and drank beer pilfered
from booths until we were silly with it. Long chains of
revelers wound through the streets like dragon tails, losing bits and adding bits as they danced to the music
blaring at every street corner, drums and horns and lutes
and jangles, up the hill and down again. There were
Town girls and School girls and Outside girls to tease
and follow and try to snuggle in corners, and in the late,
late afternoon Yarrel and one of the girls went into a sta-

ble to look at the horses and were gone rather longer than necessary for any purpose I could think of. I sprawled on a pile of clean straw, grinning widely at nothing, sipping at my beer, and watching as the sun dropped behind the town and the first rockets spangled the dark.

The figure which came out of the dark was wholly strange, but the voice was perturbingly familiar. "Peter. Here you are, discovered in the midst of the multitude. Come with me and learn what Festival food should be!"

For a moment I wanted to say that I would rather wait for Yarrel, rather just lie on the straw and look at the sky, but the habit of obeying that voice was too much for me. I staggered to my feet, feeling shoddy and clumsy beside that glittering figure with its princely helm masked in sequins and gems. We went up the hill to a lanterned terrace set with tables where stepped gardens glimmering with fountains sloped down into green shade. There was wine which turned into dizzy laughter and food to make the pork pies die of shame and many sparkling gamesmen gathering out of the darkness to the table where my friend held court, the tall Demon and the Tragamors, from Bannerwell, as Yarrel had said, all drinking together until the night swirled around us in a maelstrom of light and sound.

Except that in the midst of it all, something inside me got up and walked away. It was as though Peter left Peter's body lolling at the table while Peter's mind went elsewhere to look down upon them all from some high, clean place. It saw the Demon standing at the top of one flight of marble stairs, one Tragamor halfway down another flight, and the other brooding on the lower terrace beside a weeping tree. Torches burning behind the Demon threw a long, wing-shaped shadow onto the walkway below where red light washed like a shallows of blood. Into that space came a lonely figure, masked but

unmistakable. King Mertyn. The warm, night air turned
chill as deep winter, and the sounds of Festival faded.
Mertyn looked up to see Mandor rise, to hear him call,
"I challenge, King!"

The King did not raise his voice, yet I heard him as
clearly as though he spoke at my ear. "So, Prince
Mandor. Your message inviting me to join you did not
speak of challenge."

The Peter-who-watched stared down, impotent to
move or call. Couldn't the King see those who stood
there? Demon and Tragamor, substance and shade,
True Game challenged upon him here, and the very air
alive with cold. King's Blood Four, here, now, in this
place and no other, a Measurable Demesne. But
Mandor surely would not be so discourteous. Not now.
It was *Festival*.

Drunken-Peter reached a hand, fumbled at the
Prince's sleeve. "No, No, Mandor. It's not . . . not
courteous . . ." The hand, my hand, was slapped away
by an armored glove, struck so violently that it lay
bleeding upon the table before drunken-Peter while the
other me watched, watched.

The King called again. "Is it not forbidden to call
challenge during Festival or in a Schooltown, Mandor?
Have you not learned it so?

Answered by crowing laughter. "Many things are forbidden, Mertyn. Many things. Still, we do them."

"True. Well, if you would have it so, Prince—then
have it so. I move."

And from behind one of the crystal fountains which
had hidden him from us came that lonely Sorcerer I had
wondered at, striding into the light until he stood just
behind the King, full of silent waiting, clear as glass,
holding whatever terrible thing he had been given to
hold.

Drunken-Peter felt Mandor stiffen, saw the armored

hand clench with an audible clang. Drunken-Peter looked up to see sweat bead the Prince's forehead, to see a vein beating beside a glaring eye. From the Sorcerer below light began to well upward, a force as impersonal as water building behind a dam. Peter-who-watched knew the force would be unleashed at the next move. Drunken-Peter knew nothing, only sat dizzy and half sick before the puddled wine and remnants of the feast as Prince Mandor stooped above him to say, "Peter . . . I do not wish to be . . . discourteous . . ." The voice hummed with tension, cracked with strain. With what enormous effort did he then make it light and caressing? "Go down and tell Gamesmaster Mertyn I did but . . . jest. Invite him to have wine with us . . ."

Peter-who-watched screamed silently above. Drunken-Peter staggered to his feet, struggled into a jog past the tall Demon, imagining as he went an expression of—was it scorn? on that face below the half helm, then down the long flight of stairs toward the garden, lurching, mouth open, eyes fixed upon Gamesmaster Mertyn, onto the red-washed pave, hearing from above the cry of frustrated fury, "Talisman . . . to King's Blood Four."

Peter-above saw the power strike. Drunken-Peter cried as he fell, "No. No, Mandor. You would not be so false to me . . . to me . . ." before the darkness fell.

I woke in a tower room, a strange room, narrow windows showing me clouds driven across a gray sky. It hurt to move my head. At the bedside Chance sat, dozing, and my movement wakened him. He hrummed and hruphed himself into consciousness.

"Feel better? Well then, you wouldn't know whether you do or not, would you? You wouldn't even know how lucky you are."

"I'm not . . . dead. I should be dead."

"Indeed you should. Sacrificed in the play, like a pawn, dead as a pantry mouse under the claws of the cat. You would be, too, except for this." He picked my ragged jacket from the floor, holding it so that I could see what the rents revealed, a tracery of golden thread and silver wire, winking red eyes of tiny gems set into the circuits of stitchery in the lining. "He bade Nitch sew this into your jacket. Just in case."

"How did he know? I don't understand . . ."

"It would be hard to understand," said Chance, "except by one long mired in treachery. Ah. But Mertyn is not young, lad. He has seen much and studied more. He saw those ribbons, and he knew. Oh, if they'd been a few colorful things such as any friend might give, he'd have understood. A love gift, after all. But those you had? Nothing else like them in the town? What purpose a gift like that?"

"I thought he gave them to me so that he would know me among all the other maskers . . ."

"Then you saw deep, lad, and didn't know it."

"Did he mean to play me, even then?" I cried in my belly, a hard knot of pain there which hurt more than the fire beneath the bandages on my face and arms.

Chance shrugged, leaned to smooth my pillow. "Do you students know what you will play before the game begins? You set your pieces out in the game box, all shining, the ones you think you'll play and the ones you hold in reserve. Maybe he brought you along to see him win. But, he wasn't strong enough to win against the King, and he wasn't brave enough to stand against the move and bear the play as it came, so he threw you into the game like a bone to a Fustigar."

I think I cried then, for he said nothing more. Then I slept. Then I woke again, and it was morning, with Mertyn in the chair beside my bed.

"I am sorry you were hurt, Peter," he said. "Perhaps you would rather be dead, but I gambled you would not feel so a year from now. Had I the skill with shields and deflectors I do with other strategy, I would have saved you these wounds."

For a long time I simply looked at him, at the gray hair falling in a tumbled lock across his forehead, at the line of his cheeks and the curve of his lips, so much like my own. There was nothing there unkindly, and yet I was angry with him. He had saved my life, and I hated him. The anger and hatred made no sense, were foolish. I would not repay him with foolishness, therefore I could not repay him.

He stared at his boots. "When you were put into play, Sorcerer struck. An Imperative. Nothing I could do. The screen in your jacket was not perfect. There was considerable splash, and you caught a little of it. Mandor caught most."

I had to ask. "The Prince? Gamesmaster Mandor?"

"I do not know. His players carried him away. They do not know at Havad's House. Likely he is lost in play. He had provoked me more than once, Peter, but even then I did not call for that Game."

"I know."

He sighed, very deeply. "I am sending you away from Mertyn's House. Shielding you was forbidden. When we do things that are forbidden, there is always a price. For me, the price will be to lose you, for I have been fond of you, Peter." He leaned forward and kissed me, forbidden, forbidden, forbidden. Then he went away. I did not see him again.

For me, the price was to be sent away from everything I had ever known. It was hard, though not as hard as they could have made it, for they let Yarrel and Chance go with me. We were to become an Ordo Vagorum, so Chance said. I had put myself in another's hands, truly and completely. I had learned why that is foolish. Never mind that it is forbidden. It is foolish.

They did not forbid me to play the Game—someday. I was no nearer to being named. There were wounds on my face which would make scars I would always carry. They said something about sending us to another House, one far away, one requiring a very long journey.

I got over being angry at King Mertyn. Each morning when I woke I had tears on my face left over from brightly colored dreams, but I could not really remember what they were.

2

Journeying

I remember only odds and ends about the time that followed, pictures, fragments as of dreams or stories of things that happened to someone else. I remember sitting in a window at harborside, water clucking against the wall beneath me, the blue-bordered curtain flapping in the wind, flap, flap, striking the bandage on my head. The border was woven with a pattern of swans, and I bore the pain of it rather than move away. Chance and Yarrel seem to have ignored me then as they went about the business of readying us for travel. The piles of supplies in the room behind me grew larger, but I had no idea what was in them.

I remember Chance reading the let-pass which had been issued by Mertyn's House and countersigned by the Council of Schooltown, a pass begging the indulgence of Gamesmen everywhere in letting us go by without involving us in whatever might be going on. It was only as good as the good nature of those who might read it, but Chance seemed to take some comfort from it, nonetheless. Chance spoke of Schooltown as built remote from the lands of the True Game and warded about with protections in order to "keep our study academic and didactic rather than dangerously experiential." Yarrel mocked him for sounding pompous, and he replied that he merely quoted Gamesmaster Mertyn. That sticks in my head, oddly.

I remember Chance buying charts from a map-man, the map-man waxing poetic about the accuracy with which the Demesnes were shown and the delicacy with which the cartouches were drawn—these being the symbols mapmakers use to show which Gamesmen may dwell in a given place.

I remember boarding the Lakely Lass, a fat-bellied little ship which was to take us from the mouth of the River Reave along the north and western shores of the Gathered Waters until we came at last to Vestertown and the highroad leading south. There was a Seer standing at the rail as we came aboard, his gauze-covered face turned toward me so that I could see the glitter of his eyes beneath the painted pattern of moth wings. Then I remember huddling with Chance and Yarrel over a chart spread on the rough table, shadows scurrying across it from the hanging lantern each time the ship rolled, Chance pointing and peering and mumbling . . .

"Over there, east, is the Great Dragon Demesne. See the cartouche, dragon head, staff—that's for a warlock, a slather of spears showing he's got Armigers. Well, we'll miss that by a good bit."

"How will we know the highroad is safe?" asked Yarrel in his usual practical tone.

"We'll go mousey and shy, my boys, mousey and shy. Quiet, like so many owl shadows under the trees, making no hijus cries or bringing on us the attentions of the powerful. Well, hope has it there are many alive in the world of the Game who have never seen the edge of it played."

I said, "I don't understand that." They both stared at me in astonishment.

"Well, well, with us again are you? We'd about given you up, we had, and resolved to carry your senseless carcass the whole way to its new House without your tenancy. You don't understand it? Why, boy, it's 'most the first lesson you learned."

"I can't remember," I mumbled. It was true. I couldn't.

"Why," he said, "when you were no more than four or five, we used to play our little two-space games in the kitchen before the fire, you and me. You with your little-bit queen and king on each side, the white and the black, and your wee armigers and priests and the tiny sentinels at each end, standing high on their parapets, and me the same. All set out on the board in such array, like the greatest army of ever was in a small boy's head. You remember that?"

I nodded that I did, wondering how it connected.

"Well, then. We'd play a bit, you and me, move by move, and maybe I'd win, or maybe by some strange cleverness," he winked and nodded at Yarrel, "some most exceptional cleverness, you'd win. And there on the board would be the lonely pawn, perhaps, or the sentinel on his castle walk, never moved once since the game began. True?"

Again, I nodded, beginning to understand.

"So. That piece was not touched by the edge of the game. It stood there and wasn't bothered by the armigers jumping here and there or churchmen rushing up and down. It's the same in the True Game, lad. Of course, in House they don't talk much about the times that Gamesmen *don't* play, but truth to tell much of life is spent just standing about or traveling here and there, like the little pawn at the side of the board."

He was right. We didn't spend any time in House learning a thing about not playing. All our time was spent in learning to play, learning what moves could be made by which Gamesmen, what powers each had, what conditions influenced the move, how to determine where the edge of a Demesne would lie.

"But even if they're not involved in the play," I protested, "surely they *feel* the power . . ."

" 'Tis said not," he said. "No more than in the lands

of the Immutables who stand outside the Game altogether."

"Nothing is outside the Game," I protested once more, with rather less certainty.

"Nothing but the Immutables, Lad, and they most unquestionably are."

"I thought them mythical. Like Ghost Pieces." Even saying it, I made the diagonal slash of the hand which warded evil. Chance cocked his head, his cheeks bulging in two little, hard lumps as he considered this, eyes squeezed almost shut with thought under the fluffy feathers of his gray hair. "No, not myth. And, it may be that ghost pieces are not mythical either. In the Schooltowns many things are thought to be myths, as they may be—in Schooltowns. Out in the purlieus, though, many things happen which we do not hear of in the towns. Who knows what may be, where we are going."

I remarked wonderingly that I did not know where we were going, and they laughed at me. Not as though they were amused, but more as if they would as soon have tied me up and used me for fish bait but allowed laughter as a more or less innocent substitute for that. I knew from their laughter they must have told me before, more than once. There was even slight annoyance in Yarrel's voice as he said, "We're sent to the School at Evenor, near the High Lakes of Tarnoch." When he saw no comprehension, he went on, "Where the High King's sons are schooled, ninny." I wanted very much to inquire why we went there but was hurt enough by the laughter to give them no room for more of the same. Where had I been those last days? Well, I knew where I had been, and there was no good sense in it.

Chance patted my shoulder kindly. "That's a'right, lad. King Mertyn said you'd suffer some from shock and from the painkillers they gave you for the burns. We'll welcome you back whenever you arrive. Now, try a little sleep to hurry things along."

The next thing I remember after that is the sun, broken into glittering shards by the waves, and shouts of men on the fantail where they trolled for lake sturgeon. Two enormous fish were already flopping on the deck surrounded by determined fish hackers. I knew they were after caviar, the black pearls of the Gathered Waters, famous all over the purlieus of the South, so they say. Later that day we came to a little lakeport, and there was much heaving of sacks and cartons, much jocularity and beer. We ate in a guest house, grilled fish with sour herbs, lettuces, sweet butter, and new bread. Chance and the kitchen wife became quite friendly; I had wine; the moon broke the night into pieces through the diamond panes of the window of our cabin. And the next morning I was myself.

The world had hard edges once more; there were no odd-shaped holes between one moment and the next; I began to think about where we were going and the process of getting there; I saw the lake, amazed at the extent of it. From Schooltown it had seemed small enough, limited to the south by the line of little islands which made a falsely close and comforting shore. Out here, it had no edge but the horizon, a sparkling line which moved to stay always the same distance from us. This world edge was furred with cloud, red in the rising sun. Our Captain stared into that haze, his face tilted to one wrinkled side as he considered. "I smell wind," he announced. "Tyeber Town is but two hours down coast. We'll go no farther than that today."

He was wrong. The wind came up strongly to push us farther and farther into the lake, wallowing and heaving. Then, toward evening, when the wind began to abate, there was a singing twang and a shout from the helmsman. It seemed something essential had broken and our little ship could no longer steer itself. While Chance and Yarrel slept, and I tried to, there was a clamor of feet and tools around and above us as the sailors tried to fix it. I went on to the deck to stare at the scudding clouds and saw there the bundled figure of the Seer. He turned his featureless face to me and asked, through the gauze, if I were Peter, son of Mavin. I said no, I was Peter of Mertyn's House, without family. He stared at me long enough to make me uncomfortable, so I went back to the narrow bunk and eventual sleep.

By morning the repair effort had succeeded, and we went wallowing away in a wind more violent than before, only to sight a black sail on the quivering horizon. There were general cries of dismay.

"Pawners," Chance cried out with the others. "Would you believe it? Coastal boats don't get taken by pawners."

"We're not coastal at the moment," I pointed out. This did not seem to comfort him. As the hours wore on the pawners drew closer across the wind-whipped waters, making our Captain give up his attempt to return to the western shore and turn instead to flee eastward before the black-sailed boat. Thus we sped away, like a fat wife running from a tiger, the slender black sail gaining upon us until the ship was within hailing distance.

". . . oh," the voice came. " . . . oy . . .ai . . . ame . . . eeter." Chance and Yarrel looked at me in astonishment, and the Seer drew close enough to lay hand upon my arm.

" 'Ware, lad," he said. "I see evil and agony in this. 'Ware, Captain. Do not believe what these men say." Around us the air grew chill, and we knew the Seer had drawn power making a little Demesne where we stood. I shivered, not entirely from the cold.

"They say they want only the boy named Peter," said the Captain. "That if we give him up, they'll go away and leave us alone. I have little need of your warning, Gamesman. Pawners are not to be believed." I looked at the man with respect. He did not cringe or beg. He simply told us what the circumstances were and left it for us to respond. On impulse I took the spyglass from his hand to set it upon our pursuer. High upon her foredeck a cadaverous man leaned against the rail, another glass fixed upon us so that we looked, he and I, eye to eye. I could see the curve of his lip and the slant of black brow, altogether villainous, as why should he not be, being what he was. I whispered to the Captain, "What may we do?"

"There's a small fog coming up, lad. We can run on before him, for he closes slowly, waiting for it to get a bit dimmer, meantime calling back and forth with much misunderstanding. If the fates are willing, we may lose ourselves and run into the harbor of the Muties."

"I might have known," breathed Chance.

"Muties?" I asked.

"The Immutables, young sir. The one place that pawners might not follow. If they follow and catch us up, we are lost for we are outmanned." Indeed, it was so. The black-sailed ship had twice our crew, young and strong. I nodded at the Captain, telling him by this to do as he thought best. You are thinking that I was quite mad? That would be a reasonable thought. At that moment none of us asked why such a ship should come out of the wind in search of me, an unnamed foundling boy, half-schooled and wholly unsatisfactory in his own House. I did not say, "why me?" nor did Yarrel, nor Chance. It was only when the little wraiths of fog had grown into curtains and we had sneaked away among the velvet folds of mist, only when we heard a yell of fury from the other ship, bodiless and directionless in the half light, only then did I turn to Chance to say for the first time, "Why me? The Captain must have misunderstood. No one would come after *me* . . ."

To which the Seer, who had stood by us throughout the long flight, murmured, "You, none other, Lad. And

the time will come when you will know why too
well . . ." to drift away then, as I understand Seers often do, into a silent musing from which he would not be
aroused.

I did not know why then. Moreover, I could not imagine why. There was an exercise frequently called for by
Gamesmasters when student attention flagged in the
mid afternoon. They called it simply "imagining," and
the task was to imagine a series of moves at the end of
which some extremely unlikely configuration of pieces
might occur. I had never been good at it. Yarrel had
been better. It was not surprising then, that by the time
our pathetic fat ship waddled into the harbor of the Immutables, Yarrel had thought up at least three reasons
why.

"Mandor may have sent them. If he is not dead, he
may be remorseful and desirous of making it up to you."
I thought this most unlikely. I had seen Mandor's face
when Mertyn moved against him. "Mertyn may have
sent them," he went on. "He has decided he made a
mistake to send you away and . . ." Chance hushed
him, as did I. In our opinion, mine for what small count
it has, Mertyn makes very few mistakes of any kind.
"Or, someone may have seen the play," Yarrel continued, "when the power flew at Mandor, and may have
thought it came from you . . ."

I said nonsense.

"Truly, Peter. Some kin of Mandor may have thought
so and desires to take you for vengeance."

"Me! I did nothing to him. It was he who tried to kill
me."

"But, they may not know that. Someone watching
from a bad vantage point, they might think it was you."

"Or someone from afar," agreed Chance. "Someone
who saw or heard about it but did not know the truth.
Perhaps they think you a Wizard Emergent, and the
pawners are recruiting for a True Game somewhere."

"Where?"

"Who knows where. Somewhere. Some petty King of a small purlieu may have offered high for a Wizard. No tested Gamesman would go to a small purlieu, so a pawner would be paid to look for a student, or a boy with talent just emerging."

"But, it was Mertyn's Sorcerer, not me. Mertyn's power, not mine. Power bled into that Sorcerer for days, perhaps, little by little, so that we'd not feel it going, so that he'd be ready when the moment came. It was Mertyn! Not me."

Chance agreed, pursing his lips and cocking his head like a bird listening to bugs in the wood. "You know it, lad. I know it, and so does Yarrel, here. Someone else may not."

I exploded. "What do I look like? Some Wizard Child?" There was a moment's terrified silence. One does not shout about Wizards or their children if one cares about surviving, but no lightning struck at me out of the fog. "I look like what I am. A student. No sign of talent yet. No sign of a name. No nothing. Oh, I know what they said at the house, what that fat-faced Karl always claimed, that I was Mertyn's Festival get. Well. So much for that and that. I'm gone from Mertyn's House with no sign of Kinging about me to rely on. Now, this is nonsense and makes me sick inside."

Yarrel had the grace to put his arms around my shoulders and hug me, after which Chance did the same, and we stood thus for a long moment while the ship wallowed and splashed itself toward the jetty. Around us masts of little boats sketched tall brush strokes of stone gray against cloud gray, tangles of rigging creaked and jingled while a circle of wan light hung far above us like a dead lantern. It was mid-day masked as evening with dusk bells tolling somewhere in the fog, remote and high, as though from hills, and such a feeling of sadness as I had not felt before. Long minutes told me it came from the pungent soup of salt and smoke, as of grasses burning on the water meadows, a smell as sad and wonderful as youth in speaking of endings and beginnings. Came a hail out of the shadow, and we grated against the stones. The Captain was over the rail in a moment, talking earnestly to those he met there. The plank clattered down to let us off the unquiet deck, our legs buckling and weaving like dough from the long time on the water. Howsoever, we stiffened them fast enough to gather up our gear and follow Chance up through the lanes, twisting and dodging back upon our trail until we came to a tavern. That is, I suppose they would have called it a tavern, though most they served there was tea and things made of greenery.

There was one there to meet us, their "governor," so they said, a brown, lean man with a little silver beard like the chin hairs of a goat. He said his name was Riddle.

"Riddle. A question with a strange answer, or an answer with strange sense, or so my daughter says. She'll be along by and by to guide you south overland. We want no part of you, nor of those pawners who came after you."

"They actually came into harbor after us?" Chance's question was more curious than fearful. Well, it wasn't him the pawners were after.

"They did so. The Demon with them is already complaining that he is blind and deaf here in our land. So, we say, let him get out of it." He smiled sarcastically. "And let you get out as well. You Gamesmen have no Game here. Your Demons cannot read any thought but their own; your Seers cannot see further than their eyes will reach. Your Sentinels can make no fire but with steel and spark, as any child can."

"Your land truly is outside the Game? Almost I thought Chance was jesting with us when he said it . . ."

"No jest. Here, no Game of any kind. Howsoever, we

bear no malice, either, and will send you away as you
would. South, I think you said."

"I thank you for helping us," I mumbled, only to be
stopped by his harsh laughter.

"No help, lad. No. We want none of the nonsense of
the Game, none of its blood and fire here. If you are
gone, so will the pawners go. It is for our own peace, not
yours."

So I learned that people may be kind enough while
not caring a rather. He sent his girl child to us after a bit,
she with long, coltish legs, scarred from going bare
among the brush, and hair which fell to her waist in a
golden curtain. Tossa, her name was. Riddle held her by
the shoulder, her eyes level with mine, unsmiling, as he
spoke to Chance.

"We have none of the Festival brutishness here, sir.
These your boys need be made 'ware of that. See to it
you make it clear to them, or you'll not walk whole out
of our land." Chance said he would make it clear, indeed, and Yarrel was already blushing that he understood. I was such an innocent then that I didn't know
what they were talking about. It made no difference to
me to be guided by a girl or a lad or a crone, for that.
Tossa threw her head up, like a little horse, and I
thought almost to hear her whinny, but instead she told
us to come after her quick as we might and made off into
the true night which was gathering.

Oh, Tossa. How can I tell you of Tossa? Truly, she
was only a girl, of no great mind or skill. In the world of
the Game she would have been a pawn, valued perhaps
for her youth or her virginity, for some of the powerful
value these ephemera because they are ephemera, and
perhaps she would have had no value at all to spend her
life among the corn. But to me—to me she became more
than the world allows in value. Her arms reaching to feel
the sun, her long-fingered hands which floated in ges-

tures like the blossoms of trees upon least winds, her
hair glinting in the sun or netting shadow at dusk, her
laugh when she spoke to me, her touch upon the bandage at my head as she said, "Poor lad, so burned by the
silliness abroad in the land" . . .

She was only teasing me, so Yarrel said, as girls tease
boys, but I had no experience of that. Seven days we
had, and seven nights. She became my breath, my sight,
my song. I only looked at her, heard her, filled myself
with the smell of her, warm, beastly, like an oven of
bread. She was only a girl. I cannot make more of her
than that. Yet she became the sun and the grass and the
wind and my own blood running in me. I do not think
she knew. If she knew, she did not care greatly. Seven
days. I would not have touched her except to offer my
hand in a climb. I would not have said her name but
prayerfully . . .

Except that on the seventh dusk we came to the end of
the lands which the Immutables call their own. We
stood upon a tall hogback of stone, twisty trees bristling
about us, looking down the long slope to a river which
meandered its way through sand banks, red in the tilting
sun, wide as a half-day's march and no deeper than my
toes. A tumbled ruin threw long shadows on the far
side, some old town or fortification, and Chance got out
the charts to see where we were. We crouched over
them, aware after a moment that Tossa was not with us.
We found her on a pinnacle, staring back the way we
had come, frowning.

"Men on the way," she said. "Numbers of them." She
put the glass back to her eyes and searched among the
trees we had only lately left. "Trail following. Riddle didn't think they'd follow you!" She sounded frightened.

Chance borrowed the glass. "They've stopped for the
night? Can't tell. No sign of fire, but they've not come

from under the trees yet. Ah. An Armiger, lads. And a Tragamor."

Tossa exclaimed, "But they are powerless within the boundaries." Still, she was frightened.

Chance nodded. "Yes, but they have blades and spears and fustigars to smell us out. They have more strength than we. And the boundaries are too close. The river marks them, doesn't it?"

She nodded. Yarrel was thinking, his face knotted. "Let the girl go away to the side," he suggested, "while we take to the river. They aren't following her. The river will confuse the fustigars. They have no Seer with them? No Pursuivant?"

Chance told him he saw none, but Tossa would have none of it. She had been sent to guide us out, and she would guide us out. "We will all go by the river, quickly, before they can get up here to see which way we went."

Strangely, as we went down the hogback and into the river, I began to think of the boundaries and what they meant to the people who lived there. They were all pawns here, I thought, with no strength in them except their arms and their wits. In this land the Armiger could not rise into the air like a hawk on the wind; the Tragamor could not move the stones beneath our feet so that we stumbled and fell. In this land, we were almost their equals; no chill Demesne would grow around us, blooming like a hideous flower with us at its center. Almost, I smiled. Now I recoil when I remember that almost smile, that sudden, unconsidered belief that we and those who followed were on equal footing. We galloped down the slope and into the river as dusk came, almost gaily, Chance muttering that we would run down the river then cut back into the Immutable land. The water splattered up beneath our feet; Tossa reached out to seize my hand in hers and hasten me along. When she fell, I thought she had stumbled. I mocked her clumsi-

ness, teasingly, and only when I had prodded her impatiently with a foot did I see the feathered shaft
protruding from her back. Then I screamed, the sound
hovering in the air around us like a smell. Chance came
and lifted her and there was no more smiling as we raced
down that stream for our lives, angling away into a creek
which fed it at a curve of the river, praying those who
followed would go on down the flow rather than up the
little stream, running, running, until at last we came to
earth among trees in a swampy place, Tossa beside us,
barely breathing.

I could feel the shaft in me, through the lung, feel the
bubbling breath, the slow well of blood into my nostrils,
the burning pain of it as though it were hot iron. I
sobbed with it, clutching at my own chest until Chance
shook me silent. "Be still," he hissed at me. "You are
not hurt. Be still or we are dead."

The pain was still there, but I knew then that it was
not from the arrow but from some other hurt. I hurt because Tossa hurt; it was as though I were she. There was
no reason for this. I didn't even blame it upon "love,"
for I had loved Mandor and had never felt his hurts as
my own. This spun in my head as I gulped hot tears into
my throat and choked upon them, smothering sound.
Away to the south we could hear the baying of the
fustigars, a dwindling cacophony following the river
away, toward the border. The soil we lay on was wet and
cold; the smell of rot and fungus was heavy. I heard
Yarrel ask, "Is she dead?" and Chance reply that she
breathed, but barely.

"A Healer," I said. "Chance, I must find a Healer.
Where?"

He muttered something I couldn't hear, so I shook
him, demanding once again. "Where? I've got to find
someone . . ."

"That ruin," he gargled. "Back where we came into

the river. The chart showed a hand there, a hand, an orb, and a trumpet . . ."

A hand was the symbol for Healer. The orb betokened a Priest, and the trumpet a Herald.

"Let me go!" Yarrel was already dropping his pack. I thrust him back onto the earth beside her.

"Help her if you can. I cannot. I hurt too much. I must go or I'll die. They won't be looking for one person, alone . . ."

"Your bandages," Yarrel said. "One glimpse of you and the pawners will know."

"They will not," I hissed. I ripped the pad of gauze from my head and dropped it into the muddy water, sloshing it about before unwinding it to spiral it around my head, covering my face. "Your cloak," I demanded of Chance, taking it from him before he could object.

"Oh, High King of the Game," he protested, "take it off, Peter. Of all forbidden things, this is most forbidden."

"And still, we do them," I quoted at him furiously. "Quickly, give me soot from the lantern for the face . . ."

He fumbled fingers into the chimney of the dark lantern, cursing as he burned them on the hot glass, cursing again as he drew sooty fingers across the muddied gauze to make the eyes, nose, and slitted mouth shape of a Necromancer. "Oh, by the cold but you're doing a terrible thing."

I turned from them, from *her* where she lay so helpless beside them, telling them to bring her near the river and across it as soon as they saw me return. It would do no good to bring a Healer into the land of the Immutables. Then I ran, not knowing that I ran, not thinking of anything except the hand in the ruins, the Healer there.

The waters of the river fountained beneath my feet. The hard meadow of the farther shore fled behind me until the ruins loomed close on their rocky hill. I felt a chill, and with the chill came a measure of sanity which said, "You will do her no good if you are caught in some Game, no good if you are hasty." The truth of that stopped me. Shuddering, I circled the hill to measure the Demesne, keeping the chill upon my right hand, six hundred paces, more or less. A small Demesne, someone at the center of it pulling only so much power as it might take to rise into the air (as Heralds can) to spy out the land around. I crept toward the ruin's center, searching the skyline from moment to moment. Shattered corridors led into roofless rooms, and at last I found a wall with slitted windows overlooking a courtyard.

Of the three gathered there I saw only the Healer at first, her pale robes spread upon the mossy stones, half in shadow, half in light from the fiery pillar which rose and fell in a languorous dance. Beside it stood a Priestess, gesturing in time with the firelight. One glance was enough to tell me what she was, for such beauty and glamor are unreal, passing all natural loveliness. The Herald sat near her, bright tabard gleaming, raising and lowering his finger to make the fire move. They were within sound of my breath, and it seemed to me they must have heard my heart. Close as they were, it would do me no good unless I could get the Healer away from them and to the river's side.

Even as I struggled to find a plan, the fire sank from its dancing column into an ordinary blaze, a small campfire. The Priestess sighed, complaining, "So I build a fiery web, Borold, with none to see and admire . . ."

He rose to put a cloak around her shoulders, stroking her arms gently. "I admire, Dazzle. Always . . ."

The Healer moved in a gesture of exasperation. "You have only made the place cold. Why can't you be content to leave well enough alone and give up these children's tricks?"

The Herald objected. "Give over, Silkhands. She has made a pillar of fire and I have made it dance. Together we have pulled no more power than you might use to heal a sparrow. Why should she not do something for her own amusement?"

"When has she ever done anything not for her own amusement?" the Healer countered. "We are sent here to sit like badgers upon an earth because Dazzle insisted upon amusement."

When the Priestess turned toward her I saw again that matchless face, curled now into spiteful mockery. "You will not be content until you destroy me, Healer-maid. You are disloyal to me now as always, hating and jealous of my following." The woman preened in the fire-light, stretching like a cat in satisfied self-absorption. "We will not be here long, only until Himaggery decides that he misses me, which he will, and sends word for me to return to the Bright Demesne. The Wizard will bring us back soon."

"I have never been disloyal," said the Healer in a low voice, full of strain. Though I could not see her face, I thought she was fighting tears. "But I would rather live where I can use my skills to heal. Here I can do nothing, nothing."

I thought I would give her something to do as I turned from the slit window to approach them from below. I had gone only a pace or two before turning back in a fit of inspiration to strip off my white shirt and hang it within the window. The breeze moved it slightly there, pale in the firelight.

Once out of the ruin and on the plain below them, I put my hands to my mouth to make that echoing ghost call with which we boys had frightened each other in the attics of Mertyn's House. As I approached the tumulus the Herald rose above it to stand high upon the air. He called, "Who comes?" but I did not answer. I knew what he saw; black cloak, skull face, a Necromancer. I spread the cloak in a batwinged salute and called in the deepest voice I could make.

"One comes, Herald, bringing a message from a Wizard to one known as Silkhands, the Healer . . ."

There was a little fall of rubble as the Priestess and the Healer climbed onto the piled stone beneath him. I kept eyes unfocused, unseeing of that face, but still I could feel the pull of her eyes. Priests have that quality, and Kings, and Princes—by some called "follow-me," and by others "beguilement." Dazzle had more of it than any I had seen, so I did not look her in the face. She called.

"Come, Necromancer, closer that we may hear this message you bring in comfort . . ."

"Nay, Godspeaker. Let her whom I have named come with me to hear the words of Himaggery." The Healer struggled down the pile toward me. When she was close, I whispered, "You are to come with me, Healer, to do a thing the Wizard desires." She followed me as I turned away, but the Priestess was not of a mind to let us go.

"Oh, come up to me, Necromancer, that I may judge whether this is a true message . . ." Her voice was sweet, sweet as honey, a charm and an enchantment. Almost I turned before I thought. The three of them had no power of far-seeing among them, but the disguise would not stand close inspection, as Chance had well known. I would have to try the trick I had planned. I turned again toward her where she stood above me on the stones.

"My Master, who is your Master also, has warned me that you are not always quick to do his will. Therefore, he has suggested I take the time, if you are troublesome, to show you your dead . . ." I gestured high, letting the sleeve fall away from my pale arm as I pointed at the far slit window behind them. Luck was with me. As they turned, the breeze caught my shirt and moved it as though something living or undead moved among the stones. Once again I gave the ghost call. The Priestess shuddered. I could see it from where I stood and knew then that she was one of those with reason to fear her dead. I led Silkhands away. From behind came a frantic call.

"The shade you have raised remains, Necromancer. Will you not remove it?"

"The shade remains only for a time, Godspeaker. Go to your rest. Come morrow it will be gone." As it would be. I had no intention of letting them discover the trick. The Healer followed me, mute, until we drew near the river. I gestured her ahead to the place where Yarrel and Chance waited, a dark blot upon the earth between them. She ran toward them. I tried to say something to her, command her, but my body had gone dead, as though all the energy which had forced me to the ruin and into the masquerade had drained away leaving me empty. I felt horror, breathlessness, an aching void, then fell, hearing as I did so the Healer's voice crying, "She is dead, dead."

3

The Wizard Himaggery

I woke with the Healer's hands on my chest, my heart beating as though within them. Some mysterious message seemed to move between my eyes and hers, shadowed against the dawn sky. She said, "Well, this one lives, and he is no Necromancer. Nor, I'll warrant, was it any Wizard's message which sent you to me. Why did you bring me to her?" She gestured with her chin to the place Tossa lay, tight wrapped in her own cloak, a package, nothing more. "I could not have healed her even had she been alive when I came. She is an Immutable, not open to healing."

I struggled away from her hands. "I thought, if we brought her outside their land . . ."

"No, no," she said impatiently, with a gesture of tired exasperation which I was to see often. "No. It is something they carry in them, as we carry our talents in us. Not all of them have it, but this one was armored against any such as I."

"You could tell? Even with her dead?"

"Newly dead. If I had had great strength, and if she had not been what she was—well, it might have been done. But, she was what she was. And you are what you are, which is not a Necromancer from Himaggery's Demesne."

Chance stepped forward to offer her a cup of tea, his old head cocked to one side like that of a disheveled bird, eyes curious as a crow's. He made explanation and apology. I felt no pride at all in the trick I'd managed, but the Healer seemed slightly amused by it, in a weary way. I would have been amused, perhaps, if it had worked. As it was, I felt only empty.

"What happened to me?" I asked.

"It was as though you had been the girl herself," the Healer answered. "Arrow shot, heart wounded. But, there was no mark on you. Were you close kin? No, of course not. Stupid of me. She was an Immutable. What was she to you?"

I didn't answer for I didn't know. The moment passed. What had Tossa been to me? Chance murmured something by way of identification of her, a guide, a mere acquaintance, daughter of the governor of the Immutables (at which Silkhands drew breath). What had she been to me? I was terrified, for I could remember what she had been but felt nothing at all, nothing. The Healer caught my look and laid her hands upon me. Then it was all back, the agony of loss, the terror of death.

"Will you bear it?" she asked. "Or, shall I heal it?"

In that time it seemed an ultimate horror that I could be healed of the pain while Tossa lay unmourned. I said, "Let me bear it—if I can." I was not certain I could.

They carried her body back to the edge of the trees, wrapped well against birds and beasts, and buried it under a cairn, leaving a message there to her father for those who would come searching. Chance trembled at the thought of that man's anger following us; the Immutables were said to be terrible in wrath. We went off to the ruins as I wept and ached and drew breaths like knives into me. She had been a girl, only a girl. She had been. She was not. I could not understand a world in which this could be true and the pain of it so real. I did not know her at all; I was her only mourner. This was more horrible than her death.

The Healer called out as we approached the ruins. While the others circled it, I went through the tumbled stones to retrieve my shirt. The trickery had been laid bare, but it was a good shirt and I had no intention of leaving it there. The route I had taken on the night before eluded me; I came at the slit windows from a different direction. There was a sharp, premonitory creak, then the earth opened beneath me to dump me unceremoniously into a dusty pit. My head hit the floor with a thump. When I stood up, dazed, it was to find myself in a kind of cellar or lower room which smelled of dust and rats. The walls were lined with slivered remnants of shelves and rotten books. Something small turned under my foot.

I picked it up, saw another, then another, stooped to gather them up. They were tiny—no longer than my littlest finger—game pieces carved from bone or wood, delicate as lace, unharmed by time. Pieces of a rotten game board lay beneath them, and a tiny book. I gathered it up as well, even as I heard Chance calling from above.

I wondered afterward why I had moved so quickly to hide them and put them away in my belt pouch. It would have been more natural to call out, to show them as a prize. Later I thought it was because of the way we had lived in the School House. There had never been any privacy, anything of one's own. There were few secrets, virtually no private belongings. Secret things were wonderful things, and these were truly marvelous, so I gathered them as a squirrel does nuts, hiding them as quickly. They were not paying any attention to me at any rate, for the Healer had attracted it all. She had found all her belongings gone, Borold and Dazzle gone, and was in full lament.

"My clothes," she wailed. "My boots. My box of herbs. Everything. Why would they do that?"

"Probably because they thought they were following

you," said Yarrel, sensibly. "To that Wizard Peter pretended the message came from . . ."

"Oh, by the ice and the wind and the seven hells," she said. "They would be just such fools as to do that." Then she fell silent and we didn't find out for some time what that was all about. There was nothing for us to do but travel together, for the Bright Demesne of the Wizard Himaggery lay south, the way we were going.

We slept before starting out, I crying myself to sleep, hurting because of Tossa, saying to myself, "This is what love is." It was not love, not at all, but I did not know that then. When we woke it was with a high riding moon to light our way south.

During the way south I learned something more of women. Yarrel taught me. He did not see the Healer as anything mysterious or strange. He saw her as a woman and treated her, so far as I could see, as he had treated Tossa, with a certain teasing respect which had much laughter in it. The first village we came to he insisted we buy her a pagne to wear, she having nothing with her but the one dress and light robe, both becoming raggedy from the road. Once the people saw a Healer was come, however, nothing would do but that they stoke the oven in the market place and bring the sick to lie about it. She, all glittering-eyed and distant, walked among them touching this one and that until, when she was finished, most had risen on their feet and the oven was cooled no warmer than my hand from her draw of power from it. They paid her well, and she insisted on repaying us for the pagne, though I argued it was small pay for healing me.

"I have your company," she said simply, for once not going on like a coven of crows gabbing all at once. She was tired. I could see it in her face. "It is good to have company on the road, even pawns and boys, if you take no offense at that."

We told her we were not offended by truth. Later,

when we stopped for the night, she wrapped herself in the bright pagne and combed out her hair. I thought once again of birds, but this time of the clamorous, unpredictable parrots with their sudden laughter and wise eyes. Her hair was the color of silver wood ash, and her eyes were green as leaves in her pale, oval face. Chance was once more gloating over his charts, and she leaned on his shoulder to trace our way south among the hills. "Dazzle has gone to the Bright Demesne," she said. "She and Borold, thinking Himaggery sent for me. Oh, she will be a jealous witch, Dazzle, thinking anyone has sent for me." She sounded very tired. I thought of Dazzle's beauty and shivered. How could one such as that be jealous of anyone? Silkhands went on. "She believes she loves him, you see, the Wizard. But Himaggery is proof against her, and it drives her to excess. Ah, well, we will get there soon after her and no doubt bring her away again. She will be very angry."

Yarrel asked, "Why do you care? Are you her leman?"

"Half sister, rather. Our father was the same, but she was born to another mother than Borold's and mine. I am oldest, by six years."

"Why were you sent away?"

"Because Dazzle stirs trouble as a cook stirs soup. You called her Godspeaker, Priestess, but she is no Priestess. She is a witch, as uncontrollable as storm."

"Where is this Bright Demesne?" asked Chance. "I can't find it here what should be so sizeable."

She helped him search, but there was no sign of it upon the chart. Chance puffed his cheeks in complaint. "No trust, lads, that's what it comes to. Pay gold, or healing, or laughter if you're a clown, and get nothing but tricks and lies. This chart was said to be *complete,* and look at it—some old thing dusted off and sold with pretense." He folded it sadly, stroking the parchment with a calloused hand. I knew how he felt. It was a god-

like feeling to spread the charts and trace one's way softly along a crease of hill, imagining the way, learning the
names and aspects of the land. It was less wonderful if
one knew that the charts lied. Then it was only pretend,
not true game.

That night I lay awake after the others slept, mazed
by a lucific moon, and set out the tiny Gamesmen I had
found. For the first time I noted they were not like those
I had played with as a child. Of the white pieces, the
tallest was a Queen, but there was no King beside her.
Instead there was a white Healer. There were two Seers,
two Armigers, two Sentinels, but no Churchmen. Of the
black pieces the tallest was a Necromancer. There was a
Sorcerer almost as tall, then two Tragamors, two Elators, two Demons. I could not tell what the little men
were, crouchy and fuzzed in the moonlight. In the first
morning light I looked again. They were crouchy indeed, Shapeshifters all, of the same ilk but differing in
detail. Each piece had the same fascination in the hand I
had felt when I first held them. Unwillingly, I put them
away, each wrapped in a scrap of cloth and buried under
my needfuls.

Traveling south, sun and rain, forest and meadow,
Silkhand's chatter, Yarrel's silences, Chance's wry com-
mentary upon the world, no chill, no menace. Silkhands
said that Himaggery had taken much of the land around
Lake Yost and assembled thousands of Gamesmen
there. Chance laughed, but she claimed it was true.
How so many could find power to exist, she did not say.
We did not ask. It was only a tall tale, we thought. Hum
of bees, quiet sough of wind. Then, suddenly, as we
climbed a high ridge of stone, a cold gust from above,
chill as winter, without warning. We ran for over-
hanging stone and peered from beneath it like badgers.

"Dragon," whispered Yarrel. I saw it then, planing
across the valley beyond, great wings outspread, long

neck stretched like an arrow, tail behind, straight as a spear. Fire bloomed around its jaws. I was the first to see the other, higher, diving out of the sun. It was something I had never seen before. "Cold Drake," someone said in a hiss. The cold intensified. We huddled close, pulling clothing from the packs to wrap with our blankets around us, to keep our heat in. Neither of the Gamesmen knew we were there or cared. They would soak our heat for their play just as they would that from the sun-hot stones. All we could do was wait in the shelter of the stones, praying they would fly on before it grew too cold for us.

I wondered as we lay there how many thousands of pawns—and lesser Gamesmen, too—had died thus, lying helpless under stones or trees or in their houses while Gamesmen drew their heat away, slow degree by slow degree, until they fell into that last sleep. We had seen bones here and there as we traveled, littering the roadside, heaped around the ruins where Silkhands had been, all those who had stayed quiet and cold while Gamesmen played. Even so, it was a wondrous thing to watch the Dragon and the Cold Drake fight.

The one was all sinuous movement, twisting coil, black on black with frosty breath; the other all arrow darting, climb and dive, amber on gold with the breath of fire. As it grew colder around us, it grew more difficult for the Gamesmen to draw heat as well, and their movement slowed. We kept expecting them to move away, over the sunwarmed plains, but they did not. We knew then that they dueled, that they had set the boundaries of their Game and would not leave them until one or both were dead.

The end came as suddenly as the beginning. The Cold Drake caught the Dragon full in a looping coil which tightened, tightened. The Dragon screamed. They fell together, linked, faster and faster, wings unmoving, a blur in the clear air. Then they were upon the plain before us, lost in a stirred cloud of frigid dust which erupted into the wind and was gone. The Healer sobbed and moved into the open, stumbling toward those distant bodies, we after her. She paused at one body only a moment, then went on to the other. He breathed feebly, back in his own form, a slender youth looking scarcely older than I, pale of skin with black hair and the long ears of the southern people. He tried to focus his agonized gaze upon the Healer, said "Healer . . . please . . ." Silkhands reached out as though to touch him then turned away.

"Too cold," she said. "Oh, there is nothing to make into a fire. If we could have fire swiftly . . ." We all looked around, but there was nothing to burn upon the hard-packed earth. The youth gave a bubbling cry and was silent. I turned to find Silkhands weeping. "Too cold, always too cold and I can do nothing. No power, no way to get power. Oh, Lords of the seven hells, but I wish you were a Tragamor . . ." She sobbed upon Chance's chest like a child. Looking toward the far line of forest I, too, wished I were a Tragamor, though with the cold as it was I doubted even a Tragamor could have ported wood from that forest in time. My eyes caught a glitter there; we all stared at the procession which came. It was not lengthy but puissant, the tall figure on the high red horse most of all. I knew him by the fur-collared robe embroidered with moonstar signs, even before Silkhands sank to her knees murmuring, "The Wizard Himaggery." My eyes did not stay long on the Wizard, for behind him rode one whose face I well remembered, that pawner from the Gathered Waters who had sought me, followed me. Well, I thought, run as we might he had found me. Blood gathered behind my eyes and I launched myself at him, shouting.

The next thing I knew I was on the ground with two men sitting on me. There had been a sudden burst of heat from someone in the train, a Sorcerer mostlike.

The Elators sitting on me had not needed it, however. They had needed only their own strength and my clumsiness. The Wizard sounded amused.

"And what occasions this animosity, my good pawner? Is this the one you have been telling me about?" There was a mumbled reply before the Wizard spoke again. "Let him up, but keep your eyes on him. This is no time nor place to sort out such matters. We must look upon the bodies of our foolish young." And with that he rode forward, almost over me where I struggled with the Elators, unwilling to give up. He stopped by the youth's body and spoke to Silkhands. A Sorcerer rode out of the train and offered her his hand so that she might draw upon his stored power if she would. She shook her head. Too late. The Wizard turned his mount and came toward us again. "Oh, stop squirming, boy. You will not be dealt with unfairly," and rode away toward the forest.

There were extra horses, evidently brought in the hope the duelers could ride home. Chance and Silkhands had one, Yarrel and I the other. Behind us the bodies of the duelers rose into the air to float behind us, a Tragamor riding before each with a Sorcerer between. Even irritated as I was, I admired the crisp way it was done, each knowing what to do and doing it. Yarrel did not notice. His face was glorious. There would never be anything in the world as important to Yarrel as horses.

The Gamesman who rode beside me, one I could not identify—gold tunic embroidered with cobweb pattern, magpie helm and gray cloak—began to talk of the ones who floated behind. "Young Yvery and even younger Yniod," he said, "both having conceived a passion for the Seer, Yillen of Pouws, and having studied the madness of courtly love (much studied by them and some other few fools in Himaggery's realm) did each claim the other had insulted the lady. She, having been in trance this seven month, could not intervene. So was challenge uttered, and by none could they be dissuaded. Himaggery demands that all may have free choice, and so did this occur."

I found my voice somewhere beneath my giblets and got it out. "Which of them did the Seer love?"

"Neither. She knew neither of them. They had only seen her sleeping."

"What is this courtly love you speak of?"

The Gamesman gestured to Silkhands. "Ask your Healer friend, she knows."

Silkhands turned a miserable, shamed face to me. "Oh, yes, the Rancelman is right. I know. It is some factitious wickedness which Dazzle thought up and spread among the impressionable young. She may have read of it in some ancient book or come upon it in amusements for herself, and none will do unless there is combat and ill feeling.

"That is why we were banished to the ruin. Three times we have lived in the Bright Demesne, and each time Dazzle has started up some such foolishness. It does nothing but cause trouble, dueling, death, stupidity. Each time Himaggery has sent her away . . ."

"Her? Not you?"

"No." She seemed almost angry that I had asked. "Not I. Not Borold. But we cannot let her live alone . . ."

"I would," snorted Yarrel. Of course, he had not seen Dazzle. "So long as she has you to comfort her, why should she mend her behavior?"

"So says Himaggery," she admitted. "But this last thing must have started ages ago. Dazzle could not have begun any new mischief. There has not been time."

I mumbled something intended for comfort. We went on through the fringe of forest and out into the clear, blue shining of the lake's edge. For a moment I did not understand what I saw rising from the earth. Fogs spi-

raled from steaming springs which fed the waters. The
town was scattered among these mists, and I knew why
Himaggery had taken the Lake of Yost and how it was
that thousands could gather here.

"There is power here," I said as I felt the heat.

"Yes," Silkhands agreed. "There is plenty of power
here, and not much is needed here. There is none out
there, and that is where it is always needed. It is never
where I need it!" Her voice rose in a pained cry.

I said, "It hurts you! When you need to heal and have
not the power, it hurts you!" The idea was quite new to
me.

"Yes. That is true for all Healers. And for all Seers,
and all Demons, too. We who are the children of
Gamesmother Didir have this pain." She was speaking
of the legendary grandmother of our race. Didir was
progenitress of the mental powers, Gamesfather Tamor
the progenitor of the material ones. Religion has it that
all of us are descended from these two. I was not thinking so much of that, however, as of the idea of pain.

When Tossa had been wounded, I had felt her pain,
felt her death. When Silkhands had felt pain, I, too, had
felt it. What did this pattern mean? Understand, for
boys of my age—and, I suppose, for girls too, though I
had no way of knowing—the most important thing is to
know what name, what talent we will have. We search
for signs of it, hints, even for auspices. We beg Seers to
look ahead for us (they never will, it is forbidden). What
did this mean? Was I a Demon emergent, reading the
feelings of others? But, no, this was foolishness. Tossa
could not have been read in this fashion. It spun in my
head endlessly, so I tried not to think about it.

So, we were given food and water and proper ameni-
ties and brushed up to be presented to Himaggery in his
audience hall as soon as might be. I heard water under
the floor, the warmth of the stones telling their own tale
of power. Dazzle was there, and the pawner. When they

had been heard, Chance took our let-pass from his breast and gave it to the Wizard who perused it.

"All right, lad," the Wizard said. "You've heard the pawner say he was hired to find you, hired by a Demon and paid well for his work. You've heard Silkhands say you played a forbidden game to get a Healer to a wounded Immutable, something anyone could have told you wouldn't work. I've heard complaining from Dazzle, as usual, but you merit no punishment on that account. Now, let me hear from you. Why does this Demon want you?"

"I do not know, sir. I have met only one Demon in my life, at the last Festival, and I don't even remember his name."

"Well, easy tested by a Demon of my own." He gestured to a tall Demon who stood at his left, and that one fixed his eyes upon me. There was a tickling in my head, a fleeting kaleidoscope of colors and smells, quickly gone. The Demon shook his head and said to Himaggery,

"He speaks only truth. He is only what he seems, a student, a boy, nothing more."

"Ah. So. Well then, why did you try to kill this pawner? He was, after all, in my protection."

"He killed Tossa," I grated. "He killed her or had her killed. What had she done to him? Nothing. Nothing! And he killed her."

The pawner squirmed. "An accident, Lord. A . . . misunderstanding. It was not my intent to kill anyone, but one of the men in my train . . . he was caught up in the chase . . ."

The Wizard said, "It seems to be explained. The boy has committed no wrong except for a bit of forbidden disguise. The pawner, however, has killed the governor's daughter, an Immutable. It is likely he won't live long to regret that. We'll cry you to them, pawner. I'll not have blame laid on me or mine."

"But, Lord . . ."

"Be still. If you anger me more, I'll give you to them rather than merely cry you to them. As for you, Silkhands, you've done nothing ill except exercise poor choice in certain matters we've discussed before. And Dazzle is with us again . . ."

He had stepped close to me as he spoke, putting his hand on my shoulder. I felt the solid weight of it, smelled the mixed leather and herb scent of his clothing, and followed his glance to the window where Dazzle was posing like some exotic bird or silken cat. I saw her, then saw her again and turned sick with horror. One eye socket gaped empty. One side of her nose was gone, eaten away. From her jaw jagged splinters of bone and tooth jabbed through multiple scars, all as though one half of her face had been chewed away by some monster. I choked. Himaggery removed his hand, and the horror was abruptly gone. I reached out to him for support, and the vision returned. He saw the sick terror on my face, stooped toward me to whisper, "You saw?" then drew away, eyes narrowed in thought as I nodded, unable to speak.

"Say nothing," he whispered. "Be still." He caught curious glances around us. "Tell them I am forbidding you to pretend to Necromancy." Then he left me tottering there. I could not leave the room quickly enough to suit me. Even in my own room, I retched and was sick. When I had settled myself somewhat, I went out onto the little balcony and sat there, hunched against the wall, trying not to think of anything. I saw the pawner in the courtyard below me with some other men. In a few moments they mounted and rode away, turning south along the lake shore. At the moment it meant nothing to me. Later I was to wonder, why south? The Gathered Waters and the pawner's ship lay north of us. I had not long to brood over anything, for Silkhands came to fetch me to the Wizard.

We found him in his own rooms, out of dress, Wizard-ly costume laid aside in favor of a soft shirt and trousers which could have clad anyone. He was examining a fruit tree in the enclosed garden.

"They will not ordinarily grow this far north," he told us. "Except that they find eternal summer among these mists. We have fruit when others have none, power when others have none. If we can find our way into the heart of life—within the Game or, likely, out of it—we may build a great people from this place."

I think I started at this heresy, not sure I wanted to hear it, but he pretended not to notice, grinning at me over his beard, blue eyes glittering with humor and un-derstanding. He went on.

"And you, Healer. Are you ready to admit that your presence does nothing to help Dazzle, indeed, only makes her worse?"

"Lord, certainly I make her no better."

"Did you know this lad *saw* her?" Silkhands turned a shocked face to mine, was convinced by the expression she found there.

"But how? None can. Except you, Lord, and I."

"He can," said Himaggery, "though I cannot think why. Well, life is full of such mysteries, but it were bet-ter for you, boy, if you forgot this one. Am I right that you saw through my eyes? I thought so. Well then, it may be emerging talent of some kind, and no point in worrying about it."

"How did she . . . why is she . . . I . . ." I couldn't get the question out.

"Why is she a hideously maimed person? Why does no one know it? Why? Ah, boy, it's one of those myster-ies I spoke of. But, I don't think Silkhands will mind my telling you." He looked to her for permission, and she nodded, eyes fixed upon her twisting hands. He patted her shoulder and told me the story.

"There were two children of Finler the Seer and his

loved wife, a Tragamor woman out of the east:
Silkhands, here, and her full brother, Borold, born two
years apart. When they were still children, their mother
died, and Finler took another woman, a Tragamor from
Guiles whose name was Tilde. They had a daughter,
some six years younger than Silkhands. Dazzle.

"Silkhands and Borold manifested talent quite
young, when they were about fifteen. Silkhands, being a
Healer, was much respected in the place they lived as
Healers often are, whether they merit it or not, though
from everything I have learned I would judge that
Silkhands merited it more than most. Borold showed
flying early, and then moving, and was named Sentinel.
Dazzle was a beauty, even as a tiny thing, and grew
more beautiful than any in the place had ever seen. But
she was not fond of Silkhands . . ."

"It was Tilde's fault, somewhat," interjected Silkhands. "She resented my mother even though mother
was long dead. She was jealous of her reputation in the
town, and of the fact that I, her daughter, was a Healer.
We cannot blame Dazzle . . ."

"Be that as it may," the Wizard went on, "Dazzle
deeply resented her half sister. And, when at last she
manifested a talent of her own, it was along the lines she
had first laid down, glamor, beguilement, power-
holding, and fire—the measure of a Priestess or Witch.
Because she was a power-holder, Silkhands sought her
help in healing, for Dazzle could have carried power
with which Silkhands could have healed many . . ."

"She wouldn't," cried Silkhands. "She would not do
it. She would not carry power for anything except her
own amusement and delight. If there were sick, she
would turn away saying, "They are nothing to me. They
stink, besides. It is better if they die.""

The Wizard nodded. "So. And Borold fell under the
spell of the girl and turned away from Silkhands and
would not help her in healing, though at one time he had

carried her through the air in search of the sick and
wounded. He stopped that and flew only for Dazzle's
amusement.''

"Then came a Game," said Silkhands in a monotone,
as though reciting scripture. "A very great Game, the
armies of it massing near the place we lived. And the
Tragamors of that Game rained stones upon the op-
posing armies directed by the Seers and Demons of that
Game, but something went awry and the stones fell
upon the town and upon our house and upon us.

"And my father died, at once. And Tilde lay with her
legs beneath a stone, screaming. And the Game had
pulled all the power so that I had none with which to
heal her, so I called to Dazzle, as Borold and I tried to
roll the stone away. 'Dazzle, your mother is sorely hurt.
Give me power to heal her or she'll die.' But Dazzle
said, 'I am old enough to need no Mother now. I need
my power for myself, to keep me safe . . .' and she cowered in the corner weaving a beguilement for *herself*,
about *herself*, that she was safe . . .

"Then another stone came, shattering the roof, and a
huge tile of the roof came down like a knife, shearing
her face. Borold did not see. I saw and screamed at the
horror of it. Her mind was not touched, only her face,
and I begged her for power to heal her, but she only
said, 'Don't try your tricks on me, Silkhands, I'm all
right. Let me be. Don't try to get my juice for that old
woman.'

"And she went on weaving the glamor around her with
all her power so that Borold could not see the wound
and she herself could not see it when she sought her mirror, and so has she woven since. Tilde died. I could do
nothing but ease the pain a little. It was very cold. Short-
ly the Game was over and help came, but it was too late.
And Dazzle went on beguiling . . .''

"Then she doesn't even *know?*" I asked, astonished.
Himaggery made a sour face. "She does not know.

She leches after me from time to time and is in perpetual annoyance that I do not return her lusts, but I cannot. Would not, even were she whole, for there is a deeper maiming there than the face."

"Can't she be truly healed, here, where so much power is?"

Silkhands answered sadly. "The power of healing works through the mind, Peter, as all our powers do. If an old wound is long healed, the mind accepts it and will not help me fight it. I am no Necromancer to raise dead tissue to a mockery of life."

"So, boy," said Himaggery. "I will appoint you judge of this matter. Sometimes we do this in the Bright Demesne—appoint a pawn judge of some issue or other . . ."

"But, no," I exclaimed. "Such a one would not know the rules."

"Exactly. You have the heart of the matter there. Well, since you do not know the rules, what would you rule in this case? I believe Silkhands should go away, that staying with Dazzle only makes matters worse. What say you?"

Since there were no rules, I could only use what sense I had. Though Chance had never thought me overburdened in that respect, I had sometimes resented his opinion, so did my best. I thought of the young Dragon and the young Cold Drake, dead because of Dazzle's machinations. I thought of Mandor as I had last seen him, full of envy, ready to destroy me because of it. I thought of Silkhands and her pain that she could not heal more . . . and I said,

"She should go away. If Dazzle is like one I have known, she will not hesitate to destroy you, Silkhands. If you are gone away, then part of the cause of her anger will be gone."

"Exactly!" Himaggery beamed at me. "I need her to carry a message for me; she needs to go away. You need company upon the road, so does she, you go the same place. See how neatly it works out." He turned to her. "I want you to go with the lad to the High Demesne at Evenor. He is not half healed yet, and you can rid him of those scars along the way."

"Why me?" she muttered, wiping tears.

"Because you'll be welcome there; Healers always are. Because if I sent a Seer or Demon they would think I sent a spy. Because you are to go to an old friend of mine who needs your help and care; I hope to bring him back here with you. The High King will not want to let him go, and you must use all your wiles as honestly as you can—which you will, because you are honest and cannot think thoughts which would seem treasonable. Are those enough reasons?"

She cried, and he comforted, and I listened, and the hours went by while they talked of other things. They talked of heterotelics (I wrote it down) and an animal in the wastes of Bleer which makes scazonic attacks (I wrote that down, too) and of great Gamesmen of the past—Dodir of the Seven Hands, the Greatest Tragamor ever known, and Mavin Manyshaped. That name seemed familiar to me, but I could not remember where I had heard it before. And they talked more of that one to whom she was being sent, an old man, a Gamesmaster, but something more or other than that as well. They talked long, and I fell asleep. When I woke, Himaggery was brooding by the fire and Silkhands had gone.

I was moved to thank him. The occasion demanded something from me, something more than mere words. I took the pouch from my belt and placed it in his hands, saying, "I have nothing worth giving you, Lord, except perhaps these things I found. If they please you, will you keep them with my thanks for your kindness?" When he opened the pouch, his face went drear and empty, and he took one of the pieces in his hand as though it were made of fire. He asked me where I had come by them, and when I had answered him, he said, "There, in a place I would not go because of her I had sent there. So, they were not meant for me, and it does no good to think about them.

"Boy, I would have given the Bright Demesne for these if I could have found them myself. However, they did not come to my hand and they are not to be given away. I may not tell you what they are—indeed, it may be I do not truly know. I may not take them from you. I can say to you take them, put them under your clothes, keep them safe, keep them secret. I will remember you kindly without the gift."

I wanted to ask him . . . plead with him to tell me something, anything, but his face forbade it. The next morning we left the Bright Demesne, and only then did I realize how strange a place it was. There had been no Gaming while I had been there. I had not seen a single pile of bones. I had no idea what talent the Wizard held. "Strange talents make the Wizard" they say, but his were not merely strange, they were undetectable. Later, of course, I wondered what talent enabled him to see Dazzle as she was. Later, of course, I wondered what talent enabled me to see through his eyes.

4

The Road to Evenor

Just before we left the Bright Demesne, Dazzle saw fit to throw an unpleasant scene during which she accused Silkhands of every evil she could think of—of being Himaggery's leman, of being his treasonous servant, of plotting against her and Borold, of abandoning one whom she had been unable to compete with because her powers were pulish and weak, of being envious—childish, evil, acid words. Neither Dazzle nor Borold saw us off, though Himaggery did. Silkhands was drawn and tired, looking years older than herself, and she only bit her lip when Himaggery told her to put it out of her mind, that he would take care of Dazzle. So, we rode off mired and surrounded in Silkhand's pain. I could feel it. The others could see it well enough.

As I could feel her pain, so I could feel Yarrel's joy. We were mounted on tall, red horses from Himaggery's stable, and Yarrel beamed as though he had sired them himself. As for me, Silkhands bade me leave the bandages off, and as we rode she held my hand and led me to think myself unmarred once more. There was one deep wound which could not be healed, a puckered mark on my brow. Silkhands said my mind held to the spot for a remembrance. Certainly, I did not want to forget what had happened in Schooltown.

She led me to think of Tossa and speak of her until that hurt began to heal as well. I learned that what I had felt was not love. It was some deeper thing than that, some fascination which reaches toward a particular one, toward a dream and thus toward all who manifest that dream. She made me talk of the earliest memories I had, before Mertyn's House (though until that moment I had not known of any memories before Mertyn's House) and I found memory there: scents, feelings, the movement of graceful arms in the sun, light on a fall of yellow hair. So, Tossa had been more than I knew, and less. Even as I grieved at her loss, I grieved that I could not remember who the one had been so long ago, before Mertyn's House. I could not have been more than two or three. I tried desperately, but there were only pictures without words. Tossa had matched an inexplicable creation, an unnamed past.

As well as being Healer, Silkhands became Schoolmistress. Believing Yarrel and I had been too long without study, she began to drill us in the Index as we rode, day by day. It was something to do to while the leagues passed, so we learned.

"Seer," she would say. "Give me the Index for Seer."

Obediently, I would begin. "The dress of a Seer is gray, the mask gray gauze, patterned with moth wings, the head covered with a hood. The move of a Seer is the future or some distant place brought near. The Demesne absolute of a Seer is small, a few paces across, and the power use is erratic. Seers are classified among the lesser durables; they may be solitary or oath bound to some larger Game . . ." Then she would ask another.

"The form of the Dragon is winged . . . breathing fire . . . and the move is flight through a wide Demesne. Dragons are among the greater ephemera . . . the dress of a Sentinel is red . . . of a Demon is silver, half-helmed . . . of a Tragamor is black, helmed with fangs . . . of a Sorcerer is white and red, with a spiked crown . . ." and so and so and so. Some of the names she knew I had never heard of. What was an Oneiro-mancer, a Keratinor, a Hierophant? What was a Dervish? I didn't know. Silkhands knew, however, the dress, the form, the move, the Demesne, the Power, the classification.

"When I was a child," she said, "there was little enough to do in the village. But there were books, some, an Index among them. I learned it by heart for want of anything else to do. I think many of the names I learned are very rare. Some I have never seen anywhere in life." Still, she kept me at it.

"Of a Rancelman is cobwebbed gold, magpie helmed . . . of an Elator is blue, with herons' wings . . . of an Armiger is black and rust, armed with spear and bow . . . of a King is true gold, with a jeweled crown . . ."

"And Shapeshifter," she said. "What is the Index of a Shapeshifter?"

I said I did not know, did not care, was too hungry to go one pace further. She let us stop for food but continued teaching even as we ate.

"The Shapeshifter is garbed in fur when in its own shape. Otherwise, of course, it is clad in the form it takes. The Demesne of a Shifter is very small but very intense, and it goes away quickly. It takes little power to make the change and almost none to maintain it. They are classified among the most durable of all Gamesmen, almost impossible to kill. They are rare, and terrible, and the most famous of all is Mavin Manyshaped."

"Why Manyshaped?" asked Yarrel. "Can she be more than one thing at a time?"

"No. But she can become many different things, unlike most shifters who can take one other shape, or two, three at most. But Mavin—it is said she can become anything, even other Gamesmen. That, of course, is impossible. It couldn't happen."

When we had eaten, we went on again, silent for a time while we digested. Yarrel stopped us several times to examine tracks on the road before us. "A party of horsemen," he said, "some four or five. Not far ahead of us." For the first time I thought of the pawner who had ridden away south.

"How far ahead?" I asked. I did not want the man near me and was suddenly sorry I had not asked Himaggery to hold him or send him back to his ship under guard. "How far?"

"A day. We will not ride onto their tails, Peter. You think the pawner rides ahead?"

"I think, somehow, he knew where we were going."

"We made no secret of it."

"Perhaps we should have done." I was depressed at my own ignorance and naivete. Why had I thought the man had given up? All our ruminations were interrupted, however, by a blast of chill from above. Silkhands threw one glance behind her, cried "Afrit," and rode madly for the timber, we after her in our seemingly permanent state of confusion.

"Is it looking for us?" I asked. She shook her head. Another blast of chill came from another direction. She frowned.

"What is going on up there?" She led us toward rising land from which we might see the countryside around. We found a rocky knuckle at last and climbed it to peer away across a wide valley. Our way led there, straight across, to a notch in the hills at the other side. It was not a way we would take. Drawn up upon the meadows were the serried ranks of a monstrous Game, files of Sorcerers and Warlocks standing at either side, glowing with stored power. Wagons full of wood lined the areas of command where pawns struggled beneath the whip to erect heavy sections of great war ovens. Above the command posts Armigers stood in the air, erect, their war capes billowing about them, rising and falling like spiders upon silk as they reported to those below.

"Lord of the seven hells," said Chance. "Let's get away from this place."

Silkhands looked helplessly across the valley. Our way was there. Our way was blocked. We could not wait until the Game was over. Games of this dimension sometimes went on for years. We could not go around too closely or we risked being frozen in the fury of battle. Silkhands had no power to pull from those mighty ovens and thus protect us in the midst of war. "Borold," she cried, "why are you not here when I need you?" Her brother could have tapped that distant power. We were forced to a fateful decision which meant that we were to come to the High Demesne. Had we gone across the plain, we would have gone no further. We did not know it, but we were awaited in that far notch of hills. Strange, how all plays into the hands of mordacious fate. Mertyn used to say that.

"We'll go far around," said Silkhands, and Chance agreed. It was all we could do. And we would not have done well at it except for Yarrel.

It was he who read the maps, who found the trails, who found camp sites sheltered from the wind and rain, who kept the horses from going lame and us from being poisoned by bad food or worse water. He bloomed before my eyes, growing taller and broader each day. I woke one morning to find him standing beneath a tall tree looking out across the land, his face shining like those pictures one sees of the ancient pictures of Gamesmother Didir with the glory around her head. "Yarrel," I said, "why were you ever in Schooltown? What was there for you?"

He hugged me even as he answered. "Nothing, Peter. Except a few years during which my mother needed not worry about me. We pawns sometimes have short lives. My beloved sister was *used* in a Game, "lost in play" by some Shapeshifter who needed a pawn and cared not who it was. We are not considered important, you know, among the Gamesmen. If they wish to eat a few hundred of us in battle, they do it. Or use up a few of our women in some nasty game, they do that. By buying my way into the House, they protected me for a time."

"Bought your way in?"

"With horses. Fine horses. Paid for my rearing, my schooling. Who knows. It may have done me good. Certainly, I know more than my family does about Gamesmen. And Games. And what can and cannot happen. To most of us the Game is a true mystery. If I get back to them, I will have a school of my own—for pawns. To teach them how to survive."

"Then you never expected to develop talent."

"No. To get me into the School, mother had to lie, had to say I was Festival got, by a Gamesman. I never believed that. My father is my father, like me as fox is like fox, no more talent than a badger has, to be strong, to dig deep."

"You could live among the Immutables, be safe there."

"Yes," he replied somberly. "I have thought about that in recent days."

Yarrel my friend, Yarrel the pawn. Yarrel Horselover, my own Yarrel. Yarrel who had helped me and guided me. I saw him as in a mist, struggling beneath the whip to assemble war ovens, to cut the monstrous wagon loads of wood. Yarrel. "How you must hate us," I said. "For all you've lived among us since you were tiny . . ."

"I suppose I did. Still do, sometimes. But then, I learned you are the same as us. You want to live, too, and eat when you are hungry and make love to girls— oh, yes, though you may not have done so yet—and sleep warm. The only thing different is that you will grow to have something I have not. And that something will change you into something I am not. And from that time on, I may hate you." He was thoughtful, staring out across the fog-lined vales, the furred hills, the rocky scarps of the range we traveled toward. When he went on it was with that intrinsic generosity he had always shown. "But I do not hate Silkhands. Nor Himaggery. And it may be I will go on liking you, as well."

"There were no games at the Bright Demesne." I don't know why I said that. It seemed important.

"No. There were no games, and I have thought much about that. All those Gamesmen. All that power. And no games at all. What did happen, the Dragon, I mean, was regretted. It means something In Mertyn's House we never learned . . . never learned that there was any . . . choice."

Choice. I knew the word. The applications of it seemed small. One glass of wine or none. Bread or gruel. Stealing meat from the kitchens or not. Choice. I had never had any.

"It is hard to imagine . . . choice." I said. He turned to me with a face as remote as those far scarps, eyes seeing other times.

"Try, Peter," he said. "I have tried. I think sometimes how many of us there are, so many pawns, so many Immutables, all of us living on this land, and we have no Game. Yet, for most of us the Game rules us. We let it rule us. Imagine what might happen if we did not. That's all. Just imagine."

I was no good at imagining. Yarrel knew that well. For a time I thought he was mocking me. I was nettled, angry a little. We worked our way more deeply into the mountains, struggling always toward a certain peak which marked the pass into Evenor, and the way was hard. We talked little, for we were all weary. Far behind us in the valley were still smokes and confusions of battle. Ahead were only mountains and more mountains. I went on being angry until it seemed boring and foolish, and then I tried to do as Yarrel had asked and imagine. I tried really hard, harder than I had ever tried in Mertyn's House. It was no good. I could not think of choices and pawns and all that. And then in the night . . .

I found myself standing beside my horse on a low hill overlooking the field of battle. I could see the ovens red with heat, the Armigers filling the air like flies, raining their spears and arrows down onto the Gamesmen below. I could hear the great whump, whump of boulders levered out of the ground and launched by teams of Tragamors and Sorcerers, hand-linked as they combined their power to raise the mighty rocks with their minds. Behind enemy lines I could see the flicker as Elators twinked into being, struck about them with double daggers, then disappeared only to flick into being again behind their own lines. On the heights Demons and Seers called directions to the Tragamors and Armigers while Sorcerers strode among the Gamesmen to give them power. Shifterbeasts ran through the ranks, slashing with fangs or tusks, or dropped from the air on feathered wings to strike with blinding talons.

And on each side, at the center of the Game, stood the King and the Princes and the other charismatics to whose beguilement the armies rallied. Among the wounded walked Healers, each with a Sorcerer to hand. I could see it as though it were happening before me.

And I saw more. At the edges of the battle, beyond the Demesne, stolid files of pawns. They stood with stones in their hands, and flails, and hay forks, sharp as needles. And it came to me in the dream, for it was a dream, what would happen when the war ovens grew cold and the Sorcerers were empty of power, the Armigers grounded, the Tragamors helpless, the Elators unable to flick themselves in and out of otherspace.

What then? I heard the growl of the pawns and saw the flails raised and felt the battlefield grow cold . . .

And woke. For a time, then, it remained as clear to me as a picture painted upon plaster, the colors bright as gems. Then it began to dwindle away, as dreams do, only bits remembered. How can I tell it now? Because I dreamed it again, and again as time passed. Then, on the wild-track to Evenor I saw it only for a brief time in the chill dawn and lost it thereafter. But for what time I was cold in fear, thinking I felt the mute anger of the pawns and the touch of hay forks on my flesh.

5

Windlow

I have seen no place more beautiful in the world than the high lakes at Tarnoch. There is a wild grandeur about them which caught me hard at first sight of them and held me speechless for long hours as we wound our way down the precipitous drop from the high pass we had crossed at noon. When I say that Silkhands the Chatter-bird was silent also, you will know that it was not only a boy's romanticism that was stirred. At noon the lakes were sapphires laid upon green velvet, the velvet ripped by alabaster cliffs spread with rainbows. As the afternoon wore on, shadows lengthened to soak the green with shade, and still more as evening came so that the whole shone like a diadem of dark and light under the westering sun, the lakes now scarlet with sunset.

The High Demesne stood upon one of the white cliffs over a cataract of water which spun its falling veil eternally into the gem-bright pools below. We came onto the approach road at starshine, the gates of the bridge before us crouching like fustigars, great stony buttresses of paws in the dust and tower tops staring at us from lamp-lit eyes. We were expected. Each of us had felt the brain tickle of a Demon's rummaging, had seen the flare of a Sentinel's signal fire as we rounded the final curve. I found myself hoping that they Read my hunger and thirst and would be hospitable.

I need not have worried. There was no formality to our welcome, only a busy hall-wife escorting us to rooms where baths and food came as quickly as we could be ready for them. "The High King will see you tomorrow," she told us, making off with our boots and cloaks to see what could be done with them, for they were sorely stained with travel. She left us to hot, savory food, generous jugs of wine, and the utter joy of clean, soft beds.

Such was done, I suppose, to put us at our ease, for in the night we were examined more than once. Why I lay awake when the others slept, I don't know. Silkhands was in a room of her own, but Chance, Yarrel, and I shared a room, one equipped with several beds and large enough for a Festival Hall. Perhaps it was Chance's snoring—he did that, trumpeting at times like a Herald and betimes a long, rattling roar like drummers on a field of battle so that I woke in the night listening, waiting for the fifes to join in. So it was I felt the Demon tickling in my brain again and again, deeper, and deeper yet, so that my arms and legs jerked and twitched, and I fought down the desire to scratch. What they were looking for, I don't know, except that Silkhands was wakened by it, too, and came to my bed like a wraith, slim and white in her sleep-robe, rubbing her head as though it ached.

"Oh, they will be at me and at me," she complained. "I carry everything I know and think on the top of my head like a jar of water, but they will go digging and digging as though I could hide a thought away, somewhere."

"Can that be done?" I asked. "Can anyone hide thoughts from a Demon?"

"Oh, some say they can recite a jingly rhyme or think hard on a game or a saying or on reciting the Index or some such and it will hide deeper intents beneath. I have never tried it, and I've never asked a Demon about it.

But this digging at me and digging at me means *they* think it is possible at least. I wish they would let me sleep."

"What was it Himaggery said? That the High King might suspect someone was spying on him unless it was a Healer. Maybe they think it anyhow."

"Well, so let them think it. Good sense should tell them better, and I wish they'd give over until morning and let me sleep. Here, let me share your bed, and you can rub my bones."

So she lay down beside me on her belly to have me rub her ribs and backbone. I had done this for Mandor, and it was no different with Silkhands, save her hips swelled as his had not and she made little purring sounds as he had not, and we ended up asleep side by side like two kittens. Yarrel was full of teasing in the morning until she told him to lace his lips and be still. His teasing set me in mind that perhaps, next time, I would not sleep so soon, Silkhands willing, but no more than that.

The Seer was at our breakfast, gauzy masked and all, staring at us with glittering eyes from behind his painted wings. We sighed and tried to ignore him—or her; it could have been a her for it said not a word to us but stared and stared and went away. And, after that an Examiner came to ask us about Himaggery, and about our trip, and about the battle on the plain, and about everything we had thought or done forever. And after that, lunch, and after that an audience with the High King who had decided, it seemed, that we were not intent on damage to himself or his Demesne.

I did not take to him as I had to Himaggery. The High King was a tall man, stern, with deep lines from nose to chin, bracketing his mouth like ditches. His nose was large and long, his eyes hooded under lids which looked bruised. He was not joyed to see us, and all his questing in our heads had not allayed his suspicions, for the first thing we had to do was tell him once more all that had happened to us since we were weaned.

"And you have come from the Wizard Himaggery?" he asked again. "Who is still up to his nonsense, is he? Saying that those who are Kings perhaps should not be Kings, that's one of Himaggery's sayings. Those of us who were born to be Kings do not agree, of course." He watched us narrowly, as though to see how we would react to this. Then he went on, "And you come for what reason?" His voice was as harsh as a crow's, and deep.

"To visit Himaggery's old teacher, the Seer Windlow. Because Himaggery wishes me to use my skill on the old man's behalf, High King, if that would be useful to his aged weakness. Also, I bear messages of regard and kindness and am told to ask if the Seer Windlow would visit Himaggery in the Bright Demesne." All the while she spoke the King nodded and nodded, and behind him his Seer and Demon and Examiner nodded and nodded, so that I thought we were in one of those Festival booths which sell chances to knock the nodding heads from manikins with leather balls, five chances for a coin. Someone Read me, for the King glared in my direction, and all of them stopped moving their heads. I blushed, embarrassed.

"Ah," the High King responded. "Windlow is old. Far too old for such a journey. The thought will please him, however. He welcomes visits or messages from his old students. But—no. He could not leave us. It would be too dangerous for him to attempt it. We would miss him too greatly. But the thought, yes, the thought is kind. You must tell him of that kind thought, even though it is impossible . . ."

He turned to me abruptly. "And you, boy. A special student of my old colleague, Mertyn, eh? Caught up in a bit of dangerous play during Festival, you say, and given let-pass by the Town Council? To come to Windlow's house." He sighed, a deep, breathy sigh which was meant to sound sorrowful but was too full of satisfaction for that. "Windlow's House is much diminished since Mertyn knew of it. I wonder if he would have sent you had he known how diminished it is. No students left, these days. My sons all grown, not that I would have bothered Windlow with their education, the sons of my people gone. I doubt there is one student left there now, but you are welcome to go, you and your servants . . ."

Beside me, I felt Yarrel stiffen. I laid my hand upon his arm and said firmly, "Not my servants, King. My friends. My guides. We could not have come this way without their skills and great courage." The King nodded, waved me away. He did not care. The distinction meant nothing to him. Still, I felt Yarrel's muscles relax beneath my hands, and he smiled at me as we left the hall.

Windlow's House was evidently some distance away through the forest, but the High King was not prepared to let us go there at once. We were to spend several days in the company of his people, his Invigilators, his Divulgers (though we were not threatened with actual torture), his Pursuivants. He was still not sure of us, and he would not let us away from his protectors until he was convinced we could do him no damage. I complained of this and was mocked once more for being naive.

"Why, it's the way of the Game, lad," said Chance. "And the way a great Game often begins. First a trickle of little people across a border, a flow of them bearing tales here and there, bringing back word of this or that. Then the spies go in, or close enough to read the Demesne . . ."

"The High King has Borderers well out," said Yarrel. "I noticed them when we rode in. I doubt a Demon from outside could get close enough to read anyone at the

High Demesne. You see how it's placed, too, high on these scarps where no Armiger can overfly it. No, this High King is wise in the ways of the Game and well protected."

"And not inhospitable," said Silkhands, firmly. I was reminded once more that everything I thought and said would be brought to the High King and that it would be better to think of something else. It was not difficult to do, for the High King had done more than set his palace in a place of great natural beauty. He had added to that beauty with gardens and orchards of surpassing loveliness and peopled them with pawns of exotic kinds, dancers and jugglers and animal trainers. At first their entertainments did not seem fantastic or difficult until one understood that it was all done by patience and training, not by Talent. When the dancers leapt, it was their own muscles took them hovering over the grass, not Armiger's power of flight. When the jugglers kept seven balls whirling between their hands and the heavens, it was training let them do it, not a Tragamor's Talent of moving. Once one knew that, there was endless fascination in watching them. Seeing I had no Talent yet, they accepted me almost as one of them, and a band of acrobats taught me a few simple tricks in which I took an inordinate pride. I began to notice the grace with which they moved. Talents are not graceful. Or, I should say, often are not. I have seen some Gamesmen who were graceful in their exercise of Talents, but not many. These pawns, however, moved like water or wind on grass, flowing. It made me wonder why Talents should not be used so.

"Silkhands uses her Talent with grace," Yarrel said, drily.

I thought about that, and of of course it was true. "Himaggery also," I said. "Though I am not sure what his Talent is."

"Perhaps he is not using Talent at all."

Now that was a thought. Like many of Yarrel's comments, it was troubling and dissatisfying and went in circles. So, I thought about learning to do cartwheels and walking upon my hands. Remember, I was only a boy.

Finally, after some nine or ten days of amusement and fattening on the High King's excellent meals, we were summoned to him once more. He was doing several kinds of business on the morning; receiving a delegation from some merchant group or other, buying some exotics from a bird-dealer, and disposing of our visit. He did them all with dispatch and sent us off to Windlow's house with some potted herbs and a caged bird as gifts for the old man. The bird was said to be able to talk, though it did nothing on the journey except eat fruit and mess the bottom of its cage. It was very pretty, but I did not like the way it smelled.

The way to Windlow's House led through forest which had never been burned or cut within memory. The trees loomed like towers, vast as clouds. The trail was needle-strewn and redolent of resin, sharp and soft in the nostrils. Flowers bloomed in the shade, their secret faces turned down toward the mosses, and the trickle of water was around us. We led a considerable pack train from which I understood that Windlow's House was supplied from the High Demesne, unlike the Schooltown I had known with its own farms and merchants. We asked if this were so, and the guide replied that except for garden stuff, meat, milk, and wool, and firewood, which was cut by the School's own servants, all supplies came from the King.

The place was a day away from the High Demesne, set at the top of a south sloping valley, a single white tower with some lower buildings clustered at its foot. It looked very lonely there. However, when we arrived we found the place well staffed. The kitchens were bustling, the stables clean and swept, the courtyard gleaming with

fresh washed stones. The men who had come with us un-
loaded the train, received a meal, and went back the
way they had come. Only we were left, with some three
or four Gamesmen from the High Demesne who evidently rotated duty in keeping watch on Windlow's
House. Of Windlow, we had seen nothing yet. Nor did
we until the following morning. Then we found him in
the garden behind the tower, wrapped in a thick blanket
in the warmth of the early sun.

I had never seen anyone so old before. He was frail,
tottery, his face wrinkled like an apple dried in the bar-
rel. But, when he smiled at us we knew his mind was not
dulled, for his glance twinkled at us in full knowledge of
who we were.

"So, released by my old student the High King at last,
are you? I wondered how long he would hold my guests
this time. Last time I was lucky to get to see them at all.
He protects me, you know." He winked outrageously
and drew a serious face. "He says he believes I much
need his protection." And his eyes sought heaven in a
clown's mockery.

Silkhands laughed and sat down beside him, taking
his hand in hers. The rest of us simply sat around
soaking up the sunlight, waiting for him to be ready to
question us or speak to us, as he chose. It was very
peaceful there, and I amended my earlier thought of
loneliness. Peace, rather. Content. A vast quiet which
was not at all disrupted by the cackle of fowls in the yard
or the bustle of the laundress crossing the yard.

"Now," said the old man, "tell me everything about
everywhere. My Talent was never large, and of late it
has reached no further than the kitchen garden. I see a
plague of moth there, but not until late summer." Once
again he winked and drew that clown's face, and this
time I knew it for what it was, a cover for more serious
things, a nothing to hide thoughts that were deep as

oceans. He caught my eye and said, very quietly, "You may speak, lad. Your thoughts are not spied upon here and now. In my garden today, no Demon intrudes."

So, as Silkhands held him by his wrist and worked her way with his aged arteries (so she later said) we told him everything that we knew and guessed about the world outside. We told him especially of the Bright Demesne and of Himaggery's invitation. "He needs you, Sir," we said. "He says to tell you that he needs you, to come to him for now is a time when you should . . ."

At this he was quiet before beginning to talk in his gentle voice about the distance, the time it would take, the weariness of the journey, and of the High King. We all knew that none of it meant anything except his talk of the High King, and we all knew the High King did not intend to let him go. "He was once my student, a proud, haughty boy, Prionde," Windlow said. "He wanted my love, my adoration. What is the Talent of a King, after all, if it cannot inspire adoration? Even then, I think he knew he would be a King. But, what good is a Master who can be summoned and sent like a little tame bunwit? What good a Seer who is blinded to the qualities of those around him? So, I could only give him my teaching. He gave me respect, but no understanding. He would not understand what I so much wanted him to learn, so when the time came that he could, he held me captive to his ignorance, as though to say, 'See, I have power over this Gamesmaster! What are his teachings worth? I command his obedience, and what I do not understand is not worthy of understanding.' So, he preens in his possession of me, for others respect me and he believes his possession gives him prestige. He does not know that he possesses nothing. Nothing. This rack of bones is nothing . . ." He fell asleep with that word, the sudden sleep of the very old. Silkhands stayed beside him, but the others of us wandered about the garden, looking at the thousand varieties of potted herbs, from the tiniest to some the size of small trees. Their combined fragrance in the sunwarmed space made us dizzy.

Later there was more of the same kind of conversation, but Windlow seemed more alert than before. In the evening Yarrel and I chased fireflies in the meadow. I had never seen them before, and we took immoderate pleasure in behaving like infants. Chance drank a great deal of wine and traded tall tales with the kitchen people. It was a generous and pleasant time.

By the third day, Silkhands' work with the old man had made a difference we could all see. He was more alert, more erect, and his questioning of us was quick and incisive. Silkhands said she had made small changes in the flow of blood to his brain, had added a chemical here or there, dissolved bits of cloggy tissue in one place and another, and built small walls other places. "It is only small repair," she said. "I cannot stop age nor forestall death. It will come, still, inevitably. But the small weaknesses and pains of age, those I can ameliorate, and to do it for him is a pleasure. His mind in mine feels like sunshine and rain."

With his incisive questioning came also his own dialogue with himself. We heard for the first time about his own life, about who and what he was.

"They named me Seer," he ruminated, remembering a time long past. "They named me Seer for I knew, as Seers do, what would happen in future times. Small things. A fall of rain here. A wager won there. The outcome of a Game. The life or death of a man. As a Talent it is seldom controllable, never dependable, and yet when it happens, it is unmistakable. Well. Every Demesne must have a Seer or two, or six, or a dozen. The more the better coverage, so they say. And so I became a Seer, attached to a King. That's the best place for a

Seer. At least the meals are dependable. Well, Seers have a lot of time on their hands. Seeing doesn't require time. I began to read. Books. Old books, mostly. There aren't many new ones except among certain classes of pawns and the Immutables. I read those, too. Everything. Old books half rotten. Old books all mouldy. Old books in pieces. Old books about still older books. You would not believe the trash which accumulates in the cellars of old School Houses or in old towns the Immutables no longer use or in some old ruins. I stopped thinking of myself as a Seer and began to think of myself as a Reader. Well, what one reads, one learns, of course, and it was not too many decades before I realized that all those books were the bits and pieces of a puzzle, shards of a broken pot, clues to a great mystery. It was all there, boys, in the past. Something shaped differently from the way things are shaped today."

"Were you the only one," asked Yarrel. "The only one reading? How did you get about? All those travels?"

The old man smiled. "Oh, told small lies and begged small favors. Whenever there was a particularly good Seeing, I'd beg a boon of the King, or the Prince, of whomever it happened to be at the time." He smiled to himself at some ancient, innocent villainy. "Seers wander about a good deal, anyhow. It is said to improve the quality of the vision. And, as to your question, boy, no I was not the only one. Most of the others were Necromancers, however, or Shapeshifters, or Rancelmen. You don't know Rancelmen? A little like Pursuivants. Their Talent is finding things which are lost.

"Well, I believed that there was a mystery in the past, far back, in the time of Didir and Tamor perhaps, at the beginning of things. I came to believe there would be a document, a book, a certain book . . . called the onomasticon, the Dictionary of True Names. I came to believe I would find it, that I needed to find it. Once I could learn the right names for things, you understand, I would be able to decipher the puzzle. You understand?"

"You mean that if there had been different names for things once and we knew what those names were we could . . . know how things started?" Yarrel seemed bemused by this idea. "But we wouldn't even understand those words."

Windlow was patient. "We might. They might not be strange words, you see, only words used differently. Or, so I think. And as I read the old books, then older ones and older still, I saw that the meanings of words did change. I stopped being a Seer and became a Historian." He mocked himself with pursed lips, as though we should not take him too seriously. Silkhands, however, took everything seriously.

"That is not a name in the Index, sir. I know all the names in the Index, every one, and that one is not among them . . ."

"I know," he hushed her. "Of course, I know. But it could be there. It isn't a strange word, you see. All of you know immediately what it means."

Yarrel said, "Well, yes. Among the pawns there are vegetarians who believe in eating only vegetables. And librarians who believe in keeping books. So, a historian would be . . . someone who believes in . . . keeping history?"

"But it isn't in the Index," complained Silkhands. "It has nothing to do with Talents . . ."

"It really does," said the old man. "It takes certain talents to read and study and remember."

"Those aren't *Talents*," she said.

He shrugged. "Not in today's world, no. But, in History they may have been talents. History. Of the Game. Of the world. Why is a King a King? Why are Sorcerers what they are? Who was the first Immutable, and why?"

"That's religion," I objected. "All of that is religion."

"Well, lad, I thought not, you see. I thought that if one asked a question and then found a definite answer to that question it was most certainly not religion. I thought it was History. But then, most Gamesmen believe precisely as you do, so it turned out I was not a Historian, after all. I was a Heretic."

I made the diagonal ward to reflect evil. I didn't believe for a moment he was a Heretic, but it was the automatic thing to do. He didn't have horns, for one thing, and his teeth didn't drip with acid. Everyone knew that Heretics were like that. I found him smiling at me in a pitying sort of way which made me squirm. "I don't think you're a Heretic," I said. "I don't."

"That's kind of you," he said drily. "I do appreciate that. I wish the High King would accept your opinion as fact, but he is a very religious man. Still, perhaps if one sends enough Rancelmen into the world to find what is lost, one may come up with some answers. Now, I find myself suddenly very tired . . ."

So, we went away to let him nap in the sunshine among the herb-scent and the birdsong and the laundry-woman's slap, slap, slap of wet clothes and the far-off call of the herdboys in the meadow.

"You know, I understand what he means about words meaning different things," said Yarrel. "In the village when I was a child, when the Gamesmen marched in Game Array we called it 'trampling death.' In Mertyn's House we learned to call it a Battle Demesne of the True Game."

"I learned to call it True Game as a child," said Silkhands. "But when the stones came through the roof of our house, I called it 'death.' "

What they said was true. If it had been Yarrel beneath the whip, stoking the war ovens, I would not have called it "True Game." When Mandor played me at the Festival, I did not think of it as "True Game." I called it "betrayal" in my head. But still, I was baffled by one thing. "How does he know there is such a book as the one he is searching for?" I asked. "To send all those Rancelmen searching? How does he know?"

"Peter, sometimes I think you do not think," complained Yarrel. "The old one is a *Seer*. He told us so. He has *Seen* the thing he searches for, probably Seen it in his own hands at some time in his future, maybe here in this place which is another reason why he will not come with us to Himaggery."

The old man had been so gentle with us, so twinkly in his glances and humorous in his speech, I had not thought of him as a Seer, not even when he had said it was his Talent. Then, too, he had not the gauze mask with moth wings or any of those appurtenances which lend awe to the Seer's presence. This led me to the thought that it might be easy to pretend to be a Seer. After all, if one pretended to have visions of the far distant future, how would anyone know if they came true or not? This idea was exciting, for it was the first time I could remember myself "imagining." By evening, I had thought up several other ideas which were interesting and quite original. When I tried them out on Yarrel, it seems he had thought of most of them first, and I was embarrassed. Still, I was at least getting the idea.

The next day in Windlow's garden he said, "If I talk heresy to you, you may become tainted and some Demon will pick it from your heads and tell someone, perhaps the High King, who will feel he should do something dramatic about it such as flaying you all, or selling you to pawners for transport to the southern isles or something else equally unpleasant. So, let us talk religion instead."

"Sir," I interrupted him, "did not Mertyn send us to you for Schooling? If we are to be Schooled, surely there is some work we should be doing. If we are not to be Schooled, then we must be careful not to impose upon your hospitality . . ."

He gave me a look which saw through me to the bones of my feet. I felt it distinctly; my soles tingled. "My School House is much diminished, boy. The High King's sons are long gone into the Game, not that they were allowed to learn much from me. The sons of the followers are gone out into the world as well. There are few young at Evenor. The High Lakes of Tarnoch echo no more with childish laughter and the splash of boyish play. I know this. Am I not a Seer? Long since I told Prionde that his Kingdom would dwindle, that he would crow at last like an old cock upon nothing but a dung heap, ashes and broken crockery. So I told him, but I made the mistake of telling him why. History, I said. Not Seeing. Since that time, the visions have come, but he chose to disbelieve them. I tell you, lad, that men will believe if one says, 'The Gods say . . .' They will believe if one says, 'I had a Vision . . .' They will believe if one says, 'It was told me on a tablet of hidden gold . . .' But, if one says, 'History teaches,' then they will not believe.

"Mertyn sent you here for Schooling. So, I'll school you. Himaggery sent you here for his own reasons. They will be fulfilled. So, be patient. Talk to me here in my garden while the sun shines. Chase the firebugs of the meadow in the evening. Flirt with the maidens who keep the tower clean and prepare our meals. Be at peace. The other will come soon enough!"

So, he taught us. "Do you remember the chart of descent from Didir and Tamor?" he asked us. "Can you recite it?" I told him I could not. We had seen it, of course. It hung upon the wall in Mertyn's own rooms, and I had seen it there on the day he had warned me against Mandor, but we had never learned much about it. We had not studied religion much, in Mertyn's House.

"I want you to learn it," he told us, then quoted it off to us line by line for the first of ten or a dozen times.

"In the time of the ancestors was born Didir, and she had the Talent to Read what lay in the minds of all about her, so they named her Demon and she was taken from them. And in that same time was born Tamor, and he had the Talent to rise into the air and fly so that he looked down upon the habitations of men so that they named him Ayrman, which is to say Armiger, and he was taken from them to another place. And from the union of Didir and Tamor was born a son, Hafnor, an Elator. And from the family of Didir after many generations came Sorah, named Seer, daughter of that line. And from the line of Didir and the line of Hafnor came a son, Wafnor, who was the first Tragamor. And of a son of Hafnor and a daughter of Sorah was the first Healer born, a daughter, Dealpas.

"And of the family of Dealpas and the line of Sorah came a son, Thandbar, the Shapeshifter, and of his line Shapeshifters forever to the current time. And from the line of Wafnor came Buinel, Sentinel, and of that line Sentinels to the current time. And of a mating between Wafnor's line and Hafnor's line came Shattnir, Sorceress, and of her line and the line of Sorah came a daughter, Trandilar, a Great Queen, and of her line Kings and Princes to the present time. And, of that line after many generations, came Dorn, a Necromancer, and of his line Necromancers to the present time.

"And of the pawns who served our forefathers was bred a new people, the Immutables, which was planned and done by Barish and Vulpas, Wizards of the twelfth generation of the Game, and from that line have come Immutables to the current time. But Barish and Vulpas were sought by the Council for they had committed heresy in creating these Immutables. So did the Council claim them pawnish and forfeit and sent to have Barish and Vulpas slain.

"But the Immutables which they had made fled into the mountains and the caves and bred there a numerous people, so that when they came among the Gamesmen once more in a later time they could no longer be used and were proof against all the Gamesmen could do."

Silkhands had been writing down as much of this as she could, and I saw Yarrel mouthing it to himself to commit it to memory. That noon we figured it out and put it into a chart on a piece of parchment like the one I remembered on Mertyn's wall. We showed it to Windlow in the afternoon, and he chuckled at it. "Very good," he told us, "but learn it the way I told it to you, for that is the way it is written in the books of religion. If you think of it in that way, the Demons will not think you are fulminating heresy."

That night we were saying that we could not see what all this nonsense was about "heresy." He had not told us anything so very wonderful or different. Chance heard us and said, "Well, do not dwell upon difference, boy, if you want to stay living. A little heresy may be all right in his garden among the pet birdies and the pot plants with the guards half asleep and leagues between this place and the world. You may think what you like here, but how do you unthink it before we go away again? Hmm? And you would have to unthink it, lad, or you would not last a handful of days."

So we stopped talking about it altogether and got on with what Windlow called our schooling. We reviewed the different sorts of games; games of two, that is, "dueling," and games of intrigue such as that one Mandor had played during Festival, and Battle Games of all sizes from little to great, and hidden games played by Gamesmen for their own purposes with no others knowing of it, and games of amusement, and art games, and the game of desperation. And we reviewed the language of True Game, the labels of risk, King's Blood, Dragon's Fire, Armiger's Flight, Sorcerer's Power, Healer's Hand—all of them. One says "King's Blood" to mean that the King is at risk in the play. If the risk is small, one says, "King's Blood One." If the risk is great, if the King will be killed or taken, one says, "King's Blood Ten." I asked Windlow why we did not simply say, "King's Risk" or "Dragon's Risk," the same for all of them. It would be much simpler.

"The nature of the artificer is to make things complex, not simple," he said, his mouth frowning at me while his eyes smiled. "We invent different labels for things which are not different and so we distinguish among them. I have read that in the utter past people did this with groups of animals. One would use a different name for each type of animal. It persists still today. We say, 'a coven of crows' or 'a follow of fustigars.' It makes us sound learned. We who are Gamesmen wish to seem learned in all aspects of the Game. So, we use the proper titles for the risks we run. It is more dramatic and satisfying to say, 'Sorcerer's Power Nine' than it would be to say, 'I'm about to smash your Sorcerer . . .' " We laughed. He asked if we understood. I told him solemnly that I understood well enough. King's Blood Four meant that the King was not seriously threatened, but that some other Gamespiece might be.

"Oh, yes," he shrugged. "There are always throwaway pieces. Talismen. Totems. Fetish pieces of one kind or another. Pawns or minor pieces used as sacrifices because the Game requires a play and the Player is unready or unwilling to play a major piece. And then there are Ghost pieces . . ."

"I thought they were only stories," said Yarrel. "To scare children . . ."

"Oh, no. They are real enough." The old man rearranged the blanket around his shoulders, shifted to a more comfortable slouch in the woven basket chair. "After all, when Necromancers raise up the dead, the dead were once Gamesmen. They would be Ghost Gamesmen, with Ghost talents." At which point, just as we wanted to ask a hundred questions, he fell asleep. Before he woke to continue our lessons, the tower Sentinel cried warning to the House, and we looked up to see a cloud of dust on the long road down from the forest edge through the valley. I was standing beside Windlow when the cry came, and he woke suddenly, his eyes full of pain and deep awareness.

"The High King, Prionde, has sent these men," he said. "He has been made deeply suspicious of us. Someone has come to him bearing tales of guilt and treachery. Guardsmen come to take us all prisoner." I saw tears in his eyes. "Poor Prionde. Oh, pitiful, that my old student should come to this."

Silkhands, who had been sitting beside him, holding his hand as she did for hours each day said, "Dazzle. Dazzle and Borold. They are the ones." She said it with enormous conviction. It was not Seeing, of course. She had no Talent of that kind, but she knew, nonetheless. We all heard her and believed her, and we were not totally unprepared when the dusty guardsmen rode in to gather us up as though we had been livestock, handling the old man with no more courtesy than a sheep, and shut us within the Tower to await some further happening. Silkhands spoke softly to one of them, asking if a Priestess had come to the High Demesne. Yes, one said. A very beautiful Priestess with her brother, a Herald and a group of pawners had come to the Demesne the day before. This was enough for Silkhands. She sat in a corner and wept away the morning.

"But all they need to do is send a Demon to Read us," I protested. "They did it often enough when we were there! They *know* we have no plots against the High King."

Old Windlow spoke softly to us from the cot where we had laid him. "My son, be schooled by me. If your people taught you when you were a child that there are monsters in the wood, you would have believed them. Then, later, if a woodsman had come and said to you, leading you among the trees, 'See, there is nothing here but shadow and light, leaf and trunk, bird and beast. See, I show you. Look with your own eyes.' Though you would look and see nothing, still you would believe there were monsters there. You would believe them invisible, or behind you, or hiding beneath the stones, or within the trees somehow. No matter what the woodsman said, you would believe your fear. Men always believe their fear. Only the strong, the brave, the curious—only they can overcome their fear to peer and poke and pry at life to find what is truly there . . .

"Prionde believes his fear. His Demons tell him we are harmless to him, but he is afraid we have discovered some way to fool the Demons, some way to avoid the Seers, some way to trick the Tragamors. He believes his fear . . ."

There were tears in the old man's eyes, and with both Windlow and Silkhands mourning, Yarrel, Chance, and I did not know what to do except be still and let the day wear out. The guardsmen did feed us and bring us wine and a chamber pot, which we did not need for there were old closets built into the wall of the tower, unused for many years.

The day diminished. We lit the lanterns and sat in the fireglow of evening as the stars pricked the sky above the lightning bugs in the meadow. We grew very bored and sad. There was a gameboard set into the top of an old table in the room where we all were, and I thought it might make things more bearable to play an old two-space game with Chance as we had done when I was a child. I took the pouch from my belt and set the pieces and the little book out, quite forgetting what Himaggery had said about them. After all, I was among friends. Chance was curious at once, full of questions about where I had found them. After a time, Windlow got up and tottered over to have a look while I went on chattering about the ancient room in the ruins. Something in the quality of the silence elsewhere in the room made me look up, words drying in my mouth. Everyone was looking at Windlow, and he at the table, face shining as though lit from within. Perhaps it was a trick of the lantern light, but I think not. He shone, truly.

He touched the carved Demon. "Didir," he said. Then he lifted the Armiger. "Tamor." He laid a trembling hand upon my shoulder, leaning to touch the Elator. "Hafnor," he said, "Wafnor," as he laid his finger upon the Tragamor. He named each of them, "Sorah, Dealpas, Buinel, Shattnir, Trandilar, Dorn." Last he picked up one of the little Shapeshifters and said, "And Thandbar and his kindred. How wonderful. How ancient and how wonderful."

I mumbled something, as did Silkhands, and the old man saw our confusion. "But don't you understand? It is *History!* The eleven!"

Yarrel said, "We are stupid today, Sir. We do not understand what is special about these eleven."

"Not *these* eleven, boy, or *those* eleven. *The* eleven. The eleven Gamesmen who are spoken of in the books of religion. The first eleven . . ."

We looked at one another, half embarrassed, not sharing his excitement. Yes, there had been eleven mentioned in the books of religion. Yes, there were thousands of types of Gamesmen, each mentioned in the Index, each different. What did it matter that these tiny, carved figures were of the first eleven. As we watched him, his wonder turned to caution. He said, "Who knows of these?"

I replied, "Only those of us here, and Himaggery. I showed them to him, and the book as well . . ." I put the little volume into Windlow's hands, half hoping to distract him from this strange passion, for he looked very distraught. It did not have the desired effect. It was only a little glossary, directions for a Game, I thought, written in an archaic lettering, much faded. I had not paid it much attention. Windlow, however, took it as though he took the gift of life from the hands of a god. He peered at it, opened it, caressed the page, raised it to his face to smell of it. He leafed through it, leaning so close to the lantern I thought he would burn himself.

When he murmured, "The Onomasticon . . ." the word meant nothing to me. "All those Rancelmen . . ." he said. "Year after year, hundreds of them sent into the world, to search, search, always looking for it, and it is put into my hands by an ignorant boy—beg pardon, lad, no reflection upon you personally—who does not know what he gives me. Ah. Life is full of these jokes. Full of jest . . ."

Then I understood. This was *the* book, the one he had been searching for. At least, he believed it to be the book. I remembered he was a Seer. If this was the book he had Seen himself having, then it surely was *the* book. He went on talking, almost to himself.

"See. The word *Festival*. In the Onomasticon it carries the meaning 'opportunity for reproduction.' We talk of *School House*, but the book says, 'Protection of Genetic Potential.' We say *True Game*. The book says 'Population control.' We say *King*. The book says . . ."

Yarrel leaned forward to put a hand over his lips.

"Sir, is it safe to speak so?" Windlow looked up, dazed, lips still moving. Then he became still, as though listening.

"No. No, lad, not safe to speak so. Not safe to say what I have said, not even to those I have spoken to. I would not go from this place before, for I had Seen myself having the book here, in the old Tower. Also, I have been fond of Prionde as though he were my own sister's son. Now, however, the book is here and my love is a foolish thing, for Prionde has turned against me. Let us leave. Let us get out."

6

Escape

"Out?"

I think Chance said it, though it may have been Yarrel. We were all equally astonished, not at the thought, for each of us had probably considered the idea since we had been shut up in the tower. We were astonished at the matter-of-fact way Windlow stated it.

"Out?" I repeated. "How do you propose that we do that?"

"Why, I have no idea," Windlow said. "Though I do know that we are to get out, or at least that I am, for I have Seen myself with the Book in another place than this. I have the Book, and there seems little reason for delay if we can think of a way to go now . . ."

None of us could think of a reason for delay either, but this did not help us think of a way to get out. The guards who had been sent by the High King showed no signs of relaxing their alert stance. There was an Invigilator among them who, while not quite as thorough in pursuit as a Pursuivant might be, was nonetheless to be reckoned with. At least one of them was an Armiger, which meant we could be seen from above if we succeeded in leaving the Tower but needed to cross the meadows. We had no Armiger of our own to carry us through the air. I wondered if it might be possible to burrow under the ground and said something of the kind to the others. At once Yarrel fastened upon the idea and began wandering about the tower with an abstracted look of concentration.

"That old earth closet," he asked Windlow, "does it go into a pit? Do you know?"

"Why, no." The old man searched his memory. "There is a stream up the valley which was diverted, yes, I recall when the builders were at it. They brought it underground so that it would not freeze in winter. It comes into a tank above the cookhouse and laundry. Then the drains and the rest of it run down under the Tower, here, and the closet empties into it."

"How?" Yarrel sketched a circular dimension with his arms. "Like a pipe, small? Or a tunnel? How did they build it?"

"Why, a tunnel, small as tunnels go, I suppose. About as high as your shoulders. The walls and floor were laid in stones, I remember, with beams over the top and earth on that."

"And it comes out where?"

"I don't know." He looked almost ashamed, as though he were guilty of some obscure sin. "I didn't pay attention. Do you think it might join the stream again, further down?"

"It would make sense to do that," said Chance. "I've seen it done that way many a time. Probably dumps out into a pool somewhere to overflow into the old riverbed. So I've seen it done."

Yarrel's eyes were glinting with an adventurous spark. He said, "Well, easy enough to find out. Shall we go together, Peter? You and I? Exploring once more?" He was remembering when we were very small boys searching the crannies of the attics in Mertyn's House. The memory brought back smells of dust and sun-warmed wood and the look of bats hung on old rafters like black laundry.

We cut a blanket into strips and made rope out of that. Chance lowered us one at a time down the old closet. It hadn't been used in a long time, so it smelled no worse than an old barnyard midden, musty and rank, but not actually foul. Once at the bottom with our little lantern, we kicked away piled rubbish to disclose the turgid flow of water which crept from one side of the shaft to the other.

"I'll wager it's broken or plugged further up," said Yarrel. "Which is lucky for us. There's hardly any water at all."

Still, there was enough to make the place slimy with mold and greeny slickness on the walls. In places the old beams had broken or half broken to sag down into the already low ceiling of the place and drop clods of mud and things with legs onto our necks. The way turned and swerved inexplicably, but Yarrel said it was probably that they had dug it in a way to miss large outcroppings of rock. Whatever the builder's reasons, it made a confusing way, and I soon lost any sense of the direction in which we moved. However, it was only a short time until we saw a glimmer of light ahead and came up to an opening all overgrown with brush through which the trickle wandered out and down a little slope into a mire. I could hear the river but not see it. We were surrounded by trees.

"Thank the Game Lords, Peter. We are in the trees and behind the stables. We may go from this place undiscovered and mounted, all else willing."

I left him where he was and went plodding back up the little tunnel to be hauled up into the light once more, blinking and filthy. Silkhands wrinkled her nose at me, and old Windlow said, apropos of nothing at all, "I have always wondered how moles keep clean . . ." He did not seem at all surprised when I told them the way was clear and we needed only wait until dusk to meet Yarrel at the tunnel entrance. We then spent some time in devising a way to carry Windlow through the tunnel, for Silkhands demanded that he not be forced to huddle and crouch like the rest of us. In the end we slung him into an uncut blanket, and Chance and I carried him between us. Before we went, however, nothing would do but he must scurry around like a tottery old heron and pack up bits of herb and grass about himself, bladders full of this and wraps of that. By that time the warders were bringing our evening meal, so we shut the closet door and pretended Yarrel was within. When they had gone, we ate two bites and packed up the rest before lowering Windlow into Silkhand's waiting arms. I went down, then Chance, pulling the makeshift rope after him. We abandoned it in the tunnel.

The second trip down the little tunnel was easier for me, for I knew where it ended. Yarrel was not at the entrance, but three saddles were, together with other tack. He had even managed to steal some water bottles from somewhere. We had brought such clothing as we thought we would need, and now waited impatiently for Yarrel to come while Windlow lay upon his back making learned comments about the stars. He seemed to know much about them, as he did about everything, from all that Reading, no doubt. I could hear whickering of horses in the meadow, that coughing noise they make when they are quite contented, but interested in something. It was not long until they came, three of them, following Yarrel as though he had been their herd leader.

"There were only these three loose," he said. "I do not want to risk being discovered in the courtyard where they have stabled the others. These came after me like lambs, no commotion at all, but it means we will have to ride double. Chance, you and Silkhands take the roan, he's a sturdy beast. I will take Windlow upon the gray. That will leave the white for you, Peter. You're among the lightest of us, and it's a small beast. I should not wonder if it had not some onager blood. Still, even double is quicker than afoot."

We agreed, saddled the animals and led them away through the trees as quietly as owls' flight. Only when we had come over the ridge separating the Tower from the forest did we mount. As we mounted we heard a braying from the south, as of a brazen trumpet, but it sounded only once and was blown away on the wind. We held still for long moment waiting for it to be repeated. There was only an uneasy silence. At last we rode away in the belief our departure was yet unnoticed, leaving it to Yarrel to find us our way in the wilderness—that long way north to Lake Yost and the Bright Demesne.

We would have ridden faster had we known of the tumult behind us. A cavalcade had arrived from the High Demesne; Dazzle and Borold with it, the pawner I had escaped twice before, and a Demon of some considerable power. The trumpet we had heard summoned warders from the surrounding hills. We were pursued long before we knew of it, and we rode though moonlight and shade down the dark hours, guided by what Yarrel could learn of the slope we traveled, marking our way by the river's edge, waiting for enough light to sight some landmark which would set us more firmly upon our way.

Before we had left the Tower, Chance had puzzled over the charts so that he could tell Yarrel of them now; what lay north, what ranges and valleys. All of us knew that this study may have been useless. The charts might be true or false, true as any man's skill could make them, or false as a man's need might draw them. One never knew in buying charts what Game the maker played.

The Demon behind us could not see us or touch us,

therefore he could not pick out our thoughts from the countryside. He could only throw his net into the void to skim whatever vagrant pulses were there, to recognize fear, perhaps, or some thought of the pursuer in the mind of the pursued which would tell him that those he sought were in one direction only. Though we did not know it, he did not find us for some time, for we had dropped below the rocky ridge of hills, out of his line of search. Then, at the bottom of the first long slope, we dropped down once more into a maze of little canyons which twined themselves down the long incline like a twisted rope, joining and rejoining among high, flood-washed walls. Once we were into the twisting way we were doubly hidden. He had to leave the search and climb the highest mountain to our west in order to Read us. Once he had done so, however, he found us soon enough, and the pursuers came behind us at twice our speed.

Morning came. We stopped to eat the little food we had brought, and when Yarrel laid the old man down, his eyes opened in surprised alertness. "I see," he said. "They are coming behind us. We are pursued." There was almost panic in his voice.

Silkhands shook him gently, touched his face. "Have you Seen our arrival at the Bright Demesne? Have you Seen us with Himaggery?"

He nodded, still in surprise and with something of shame. "I have seen myself there, dearest girl. So, I assumed . . . Oh, wrong to assume. Wicked to do so. Having seen myself in safety, I did not think for you, not any of you. How vain and mean to let you come this way with so little protection . . ."

We hushed him, comforted him, but I was fearful. They might pursue him, true, but I thought he needed fear little more than being taken back to his garden and his birds. Me? Well, someone wanted me for something, but I did not think I had offended anyone enough that I was seriously in danger. But Silkhands was another matter. Her fate would be a dire one, denounced by her envious sister, accused of treachery by sister and brother to one who would kill at a word and mourn his error later. Windlow had been right. The High King was a bare, hard man who would believe his fear first. I did not want Silkhands lost to him.

Windlow pulled himself together and we made plans, hasty plans, plans with perhaps too little chance of success. Still, it was better than doing nothing and falling meekly into their claws. It was decided that we would split up, each horse would take a separate way down the twisting canyons. As we went, we would each concentrate on playing a game of two-space-jumper in our heads. It was an infants' game, one we all knew, played with two Armigers on an otherwise empty board. If we could keep our concentration clean, uncorrupted by other thought or fear, the Demon following us could not tell us apart. We would all be alike to him, and perhaps the searchers would split up, as well, or failing that, would choose one way and ignore the others.

Then, when we had gone in this way until noon—and it would not be easy to keep only those thoughts for so long a time—we would sit quietly upon the slope of the canyon, wherever we happened to be, chew a certain leaf which Windlow gave us, and "become as one with wind and leaf." I had no great confidence in being able to do this, but Windlow said the herb would do it if we did not fight it. "Let go," he said. "Let everything go. And if you are pursued, they will lose you and pass you by."

If we did it well, there was a chance the pursuit would pass us by and we could hide behind them, protected from their searching minds by a thousand rocky walls. This was the hasty plan, depending much upon luck and resolution rather than on skill, for we had no practice of this deep meditation while the hunters came after us on swift feet.

"Ill prepared or no, we must go on," said Windlow. "If we had waited another day, we could not have escaped at all. We *must* go on." So we did. Yarrel and Windlow went down the middle way, the widest and smoothest. Chance and Silkhands took the western branch, narrow and deep. I went down the easternmost way. If the chart told true, all these ways would spill into the Long Valley sooner or later and we would meet there if we met at all. As we left one another, I was not at all confident of it, and Yarrel's half-pitying glance over his shoulder at me did little to reassure me.

My way led among rocky heaps full of whistling burrowers who marked my passage with alarm sounds. I paid them no attention, being intent upon the Armiger game, jump by jump, trying to keep the whole board in my head and remember which squares had been ticked off. This thought had to be interrupted only a few times to remind the horse that he was expected to keep moving. Once or twice I checked the place of the sun in the sky. I lost myself in the game, truly, able to keep that and only that in mind far better than I would have thought possible.

So—I did something foolish. Only later did I realize what it had been. The canyon I was in was a twisting one. The sun was only a little before noon, in the corner of my right eye. Much later, oh, much, much later I caught it still in the corner of my right eye and said to myself, see, the very sun is standing still. It had not. Nor had I. The way had turned upon itself, the sun had moved past noon, and I was still thinking the Armiger game in my head. It took a moment to realize what had happened. By then, of course, mine had been the only mind which the pursuers could have followed for a very long time.

I knew it was probably too late to do any good, but losing myself in the herb and the silence could at least do no further harm. If anyone had been Reading during the past hour, only my thoughts would have been there. Perhaps I had decoyed some pursuit away from the others. I tried to convince myself this was a good thing if it had happened. The white horse and I went up the slope to hide among the trees where I sat beneath a fragrant, needled tree and chewed Windlow's leaves, concentrating the while upon the grasses around me which moved so gently in the sun and air. In a little time it was as though the world dropped away, and I was me no longer. I was grass. I was air, perhaps, as well, but certainly grass, moved by the wind, gloriously green and flexible in the sun. So time passed and I was not.

Even as I became the grass upon the hillside, they came down the canyon after me. All the others had vanished at noon, gone into nothingness. I had not. The Demon had tracked me as a fustigar does a bunwit. They came down the canyon below me, would have gone on by me into the great valley without seeing me, precisely as planned. Except for the little, white horse.

From wherever I was, whatever I was, the noise of the little horse was no more than a bird call, a beast cry, a little "whicker, whicker, here I am, abandoned and left all alone upon the hillside . . ." The noise which followed, however, was more than that; shouting, calling of men, whistles blown shrill into echoes. Something deep within me wrenched, and I was myself upon the hillside as men clambered toward me. The little white horse had been lonely, no doubt, had thought himself abused, had called out to the mounts of the men who passed below. At that moment somewhere deep inside me it seemed that I knew a way of escape but had forgot-

ten it. I longed to become as the grass again, then
mocked myself for so foolish a desire. No matter how
convinced my mind might be, the men would see me for
what I really was. All this occurred to me within sec-
onds, and without abating that strange notion that
escape was there, within reach, if I could only remember . . .

And then they surrounded me. Dazzle was there,
Borold fiercely smiling, the lean and villainous pawner,
and a Demon. Now I knew the Demon. I had seen him
last on Festival night in School Town: Mandor's friend
from Bannerwell. I was not afraid, only confused. What
could this assemblage want with me? Despite all
Yarrel's imaginings, I could not be convinced that I was
the real object of their search, could not be, would not
be.

Part of the puzzle unraveled at once. The expression
of fury on Dazzle's face told me that I had not been her
quarry. She was infuriated that Silkhands was not with
me, demanded to know where she was. My thoughts
said, gone, down the valley, safe to Himaggery's. So I
thought, and so they believed. Why should they not? I
believed it. Some in the train had been sent in search for
old Windlow. I put my head into my hands and thanked
the Gamelords that Silkhands was well gone. If she had
been found with Windlow, the two escaping together, it
would have been considered proof enough of that
treachery which the High King so feared. What did it really matter if his old teacher ran away to a better place?
It did not, save to the High King, and for no good reason. I turned my thoughts from this as they clambered
around me and over me, searching the rocks and trees,
sure that the others were not there and yet bound to
search for them, bound by the same terror which
chained the High King. Doubt. Doubt and more doubt.
Fear and more fear. I sighed. The little white horse

whickered at me, and I cursed him and his lineage for several generations.

I sat in the landwrack of my dreams and cursed a horse, doing the dreams no good and the horse no harm. So it is with much of life, as old Windlow had said, a jest. We stand at the side of the board and are overrun by the Game of others. When I was younger, I would not have believed that.

7

Mandor Again

There was a shrill, hissing argument among the Demon, the pawner, and Dazzle. Dazzle, backed by Borold and the High King's men, demanded aid in seeking Silkhands. The Demon refused. Silkhands was no part of his bother. The pawner, meantime, felt ill used since he had not been paid for finding me. Of the three, the only one with any dignity was the Demon, and him I could almost have admired though, at last, even his patience broke upon the shoals of Dazzle's temper.

"If you would dispute, then ride with me to Bannerwell, for it is not my will I do, but the will of another. If you would dispute, then bring your disputation to Bannerwell and submit them there to my Lord and Prince, Mandor."

Ah, said my inner self, so he is not dead after all. I waited for love to well up in me, for gladness to occur, for some emotion to flow as it had used to do and felt nothing. Within was only the memory of grass and wind and a longing for peace. Well, I said to myself, you are tired after all. Tired from all that riding and concentration. Later you will feel something. I saw Dazzle, still screaming at the Demon, saw her real face, at which I shuddered, gulped, so deeply sick I had to put my head between my feet to gulp for air. The pawner mocked at me.

"Well, boy, and what is it with you? You need fear

nothing. They mean you no harm."

I told him I knew, I knew, but the feeling of sickness and sorrow did not abate even when we had mounted and ridden off along the twisting canyon in its winding way north. Some good spirit was with me, for I did not think of the others at all but only of my own internal miseries. As a result, the others were not further sought. Wherever they were, they escaped the notice of my captors, and when we reached the long, east-west valley Dazzle and Borold turned eastward and left us. I did not notice they were gone as we turned west and rode up into the hills. It was a winding way, a climbing way, but it was definitely a road leading up and over the high scarp which was the southeasterly end of the Hidaman Mountains, those most lofty of peaks, tonsured in ice, beyond which lay Bannerwell. The setting of the High Demesne in the same range had been beautiful, but the way we traveled was simply wild; fearsome, grim and deep the chasms, remote and chill the peaks. I was glad of the road and felt that the white horse would be punished enough by the time we arrived anywhere. So, that first day while I rode I did not think of anything at all.

At about sunset we reached a way station where horses were kept. I was chained. I had never been manacled before, and I did not like it. They did nothing more than link my ankles with light bonds and that to a tree, but it made me feel less than human. When I complained, the Demon was half kindly about it. "It is only for your own protection," he said. "You are not with us of your own free will, after all. You might decide to wander away in the night. If you were to end up in these mountains alone, well—there are beasts, quadrumanna, chasms. We mean you no harm, and you will be safer with us."

They fed me well. There was water from the snow melt which smelt of pine, fragrant as tea. There were camp buns baked in the ashes and slices of meat from the day's hunt. The Armiger had brought down a small, hoofed animal which I did not know. The beast was called "Mountain zeller," but the meat was named "thorp."

I thought I would not sleep, not for a moment, and woke in the chill dawn thinking that only moments had passed. I had slept the whole night, not feeling the chain, so tired that nothing had moved me during the black hours. So, I thought some about Silkhands and Windlow, wondering if they were well and had gone far on the road to the Bright Demesne. The Demon gave me a puzzled glance, as though what I thought of was not what he expected. Well, what did he expect? I did not even know why I was sought, much less what expectations they might hold. Nothing would be lost in trying to find out. When we were on the way, I kicked the white horse into a clumsy canter and came up to the Demon's side. It was like riding beside a giant. The horse he had taken from the way station was one of those great, feather-footed monsters Yarrel had known at once as Bannerwell bred. I felt that running so dwarfed was good for the white horse. An exercise in humility. I had not yet forgiven him.

"I would feel less distressed, sir, if you could tell me why I was sought? Why we are going to Bannerwell? I have done nothing to warrant enmity from anyone . . ." I let my voice trail off, not quite pleadingly. His jaw was set, and for a moment I thought he would not answer me at all. Then he did, grudgingly.

"You are not sought in enmity, boy. Were you not close friend to my Prince Mandor? Did you know he was hurt?" He cast a curious glance at me out of the corner of his eye, almost covert, as though to see what I thought of that.

"I was told so." It seemed wisest not to say much. "I, too, was hurt." I would not have been human had my voice not hinted asperity. Had it not been for Mertyn, I would have been more than hurt. I would have been damn near killed.

He jerked angrily, the little muscles along his jaw bunching and jumping as though he were chewing on something tough. "Yes. Well, you are better healed than he. There were no Healers in the Schooltown during Festival. It was long before one could be found and longer yet before we found one who was competent." The little muscle jumped, jumped. "He is not healed of his hurt. Perhaps you can aid him in that."

"I am no Healer!" I said in astonishment. "So far, I'm nothing at all."

Jump, jump went his jaw, face turned from me, stony. At last, "Well, your presence may comfort him. As a friend. He has need of his friends."

I could not stop the thought. It bloomed angrily in me as fire blooms on grassland. "He who sought my death claims my friendship! A fine friend indeed!" The Demon caught it, had been waiting for it. He could not have missed it, and he looked down at me out of a glaring face, eyes like polished stone set into that face, enmity and anger wished upon me. I felt it like a blow and shuddered beneath it.

"You were friends once, boy. Remember it. Remember it well, and be not false to what once was. Or regret be thy companion . . ." He spurred his horse and went on before me. I did not see him again until we camped that night. Then he was as before, calm, but did not speak to me nor I to him. In his absence I had thought of Mandor, of how I had once felt about Mandor. No echo of that feeling remained. It was impossible to remember what once had been. For the first time I began to be afraid.

By the time we had come over the last of the high passes of the Hidamans and down the last stretch of road to

Bannerwell, I was more frightened yet. I had also forgiven the white horse. He had carried me without complaint or balk, growing noticeably thinner in the process. The sight of my own hand and wrist protruding from my sleeve for a handsbreadth told me some of the reason. While mind and emotion may have been disturbed by all the journeys since Schooltown, body had gone on growing. Measuring my trouser legs against my shins, I guessed myself a full hand higher than when we had left Mertyn's House. My hand shook as I lengthened the leathers to a more appropriate stretch, and my eyes brooded over the close-knotted forest of oaks which fell away from us down the long hills to Bannerwell itself, a fortress upon a cliff, surrounded on three sides by the brown waters of a river.

"The River Banner," said the Demon, reading my question before it was asked. "From which Bannerwell takes its name. The ancient well lies within the fortress walls, sweet water for harsh times, so it is said." He cast me one of his enigmatic looks before rounding up the train with his eyes, counting the men off, arranging us all to his satisfaction. I noted the silence among the retainers, the gravity each seemed to show at our approach. The Demon said, "I was to have returned with you a season ago, boy. I rode from this place due east on a straight road to Schooltown only to find you gone."

I knew he could Read my question, but I felt less invaded if I asked it aloud. "Why, sir Demon? It is not for friendship. You know that as well as I. Won't you tell me why?"

For a time I thought he would not answer as he had not when I had asked before. This time, however, he parted reluctant lips and said, "Because of your mother, boy."

"I have none. I am Festival born." I felt the deep tickle in my head as I said it and knew that he had plunged deep enough into me to Read my inmost thoughts. His face changed, half angry, half frustrated.

"You have. Or had. Her name is Mavin Manyshaped, and she is full sister to Mertyn, *King* Mertyn in whose House you schooled. I Read it in Mertyn's mind at the Festival. There is no mistake. He saw you at risk and knew you for close kin in that moment. He called you thalan, sister's son."

Turmoil. We approached Bannerwell, but it was someone else seeing those walls through my eyes; someone else heard the thud of the bridge dropping across the moat, the screeching rattle of chains drawing the screen-gates upward to let us through. I suppose mind saw and heard, but *I* did not. Inside me was only a whirling pool of black and bright, drawing me down into it, full of some darting gladnesses and more many-toothed furies, voiced and silent, leaving me virtually unaware of the world outside. There was only an impression of lounging gamesmen in the paved courtyard; the gardens glimpsed through gates of knotted iron, light falling through tall windows to lay jeweled patterns on dark, gleaming wood. The smell of herbs. And meat and flowers and horses, mingled. Someone said, "What's wrong with him?" and the Demon answered, "Leave him a while. He has been surprised."

Surprised. Well. That is a word for it. Astonished, perhaps. Shocked. Perhaps that word was best, for it was like a tingling half deadness in which nothing connected to anything else. I think I fell asleep—or, perhaps, merely became unconscious. Much later, long after the lamps were lit, I realized that I, Peter, was sitting against a wall in an alcove half behind a thick curtain. The shadow of a halberd lay on the floor before me, and I looked at it for a long, long time trying to decide what it was. Then the word came, halberd, and with it the knowledge of myself and where I was. Someone was standing just outside the alcove; beyond was the dining hall of Bannerwell full of tumult and people coming and going, smells of food, servants carrying platters and flagons. Well. I watched them for some time without curiosity until one of them saw me and went running off to tell someone. Then it was the Demon standing over me, reaching down with rough hands to turn my face upward.

"I did not know it would take you so. I had hoped you knew—that you are thalan to Mertyn, as Mandor is to me . . ."

Thalan. Full sister's son. The closest kin except for mother and child were thalani. The Demon was tickling at my mind and finding nothing, as usual. I almost laughed. If I could not tell what I was thinking, how could he?

He said, "Do you often do this? This going blank and sitting staring at nothing?"

"Sometimes," I admitted from a dry throat. It was true. Whenever things happened which were too complex, too much to bear, there was an empty interior space into which I could go, a place of vast quiet. I seldom had any recollection of it afterward. Perhaps it was not the kind of place one could remember, only a sort of featureless emptiness. I resented his question.

Perhaps the resentment showed, for he made a face. "I can remember that feeling from my own youth, lad. There is little enough we can do until our Talent manifests itself. Before that, there is always the fear that there will be no Talent at all." I nodded, and he went on. "I remember it well. When we are impotent to do anything consequential, it seems better not to exist than to live in such turmoil. If I were not thalan to Mandor, if he were not dear to me as my own soul, I would pity you and let you go. But, I cannot."

"What good will it do to keep me here?" I begged. "I have no power. You tell me I am the son of a Shapeshifter, a famous one at that, one whose name I know. You tell me this and I must believe you, but it does you no good. I have no such power, and if I had, what would it profit you?"

"Perhaps nothing. Perhaps it is no more than a mad idea born out of pain. I have said you will not be harmed, you will not. But Mandor has it in his head you can help him, or get help for him. It may be you can do nothing, and the whole matter will be forgotten, but for now I have done what he begged of me. I have brought you to Bannerwell where hospitality awaits you. Let Mandor himself tell you more . . ."

I had to be satisfied with that. Mandor was not in the dining hall. He was not waiting for me in the room I was given, nor was he in the kitchens in the morning when the Demon and I took early meal together. The Demon asked me to call him Huld, and I did so with some reluctance. We went together up the River Banner to a horse breeder's farm to fetch two animals for the fortress stables, and Mandor was not with us. During all this ride, I longed for Yarrel and was as lonely as I have ever been in my life. Huld was garrulous, a little, trying to make me comfortable, to make me feel relaxed and kindly. I could not. The warmth came no nearer me than the length of his glance, covert and measuring. I did not feel him in my head that day, but I knew I could not prevent his Reading me when he chose. I thanked the Game-lords I was a clumsy boy, a bobble-head, a dreamer with no Talent. If he found my dreams, I would hate it. It would be like being taken for sex, without consent, but he could hurt no one else with what I knew or dreamed, for I knew so little.

To realize that one knows nothing, that one is help-less, that one's highest hope is to be ravished alone with-out injury to others, that is a lonely feeling. Then even that hope was taken from me.

"I have long admired King Mertyn," said Huld. "He would be sorry to know his mind betrayed you into a

Game against your will . . ."

So that was my value! That in my destruction, Mertyn
might be wounded! I laughed, a sound like a bray, and
Huld turned his face to me, full of surprise and sudden
offense. "No, lad. No, I swear. Such a thought had not
occurred to me, nor to Mandor . . ."

I brayed again, and when we returned to the fortress I
went to the room they had given me and curled on the
bed, willing myself to silence. If it were possible, I
would have willed myself to death. I felt the tickle in my
head and paid it no attention. Let him seek my misery
and find it. Let him feel it and know I did not believe
him. I think I may have cried like a child. At last I slept.

And in the morning I saw Mandor again.

8

Hostage

He was in a tower room, a room not unlike the one
Mertyn had occupied in Schooltown, windowed and
well lit. Mandor, however, was surrounded with a luxu-
ry which Mertyn would not have allowed: carpets of
deep plush, couches and heavy draperies to shut out the
evening cold. Mandor's familiar form was posed against
the jeweled light of an eastern window. I saw his profile,
more familiar to me than my own, the long lashes lying
upon his silken cheek, mouth curved into that sensuous
bow, his long, elegant hand stroking the silk of his
gown. Huld spoke from behind me, "Peter is here,
Mandor." No answer. It might have been a form of wax
or marble which stood against the light. I waited to feel
something and felt nothing.

Until he turned.

Then I thought there had been a masquerade, and
they had put Dazzle into Mandor's clothes, for the face
which looked at me was one I had seen before, hideous,
a gap-faced monstrosity, a noseless, cheekless horror.
Vomit boiled into my throat, and I turned away, feeling
the Demon's intrusion into my mind, hearing him say,
"He sees you, Mandor." I heard a sob, as well, and
knew it came from the Prince.

"How?" The word was almost gargled, and my brain
formed the unwelcome image of shattered teeth and
tongue bending and probing to form articulate speech.
"How?"

"He doesn't know." There was a silence during which I swallowed and swallowed, staring at the stones of the wall, not thinking. "Truly, Mandor. He does not know. He simply sees you, that's all."

"Talen'. Bahr?"

"Not any Talent or Power he knows of."

"I was some time among the Immutables," I said, bitterly. "Perhaps I have caught it from them."

"It is not unknown," Huld said to Mandor. "There are some who cannot be beguiled. Or who can be beguiled for a time, but not thereafter. You know it is true."

I turned to confront the horror, but he had turned away, and it was only that matchless profile which I saw. The lips moved. "Nus helb . . ."

"I have told Peter he must help, Mandor. If he can."

"I would help you if I could," I choked. "I would help anyone like you, if I could. But there is nothing I can do. I cannot see you as once I did, feel for you as once I did. I have no Talent, no Power. I have learned from Huld that I am a Shapeshifter's son, but I do not know how that would help you."

"Get her here!" The three words were perfectly clear, not at all garbled.

I laughed. "Get her here? Mavin? For my sake? I've never seen her. I don't know her. If I did, what then?"

"Go out, boy," said Huld, opening the door for me. "Now that Mandor has seen you, and you him, we need to talk, we kindred. I'll come to you later."

I brayed again, that meaningless laugh, that pawn's laugh at the foolishness and stupidity of the world, and I went out into the gardens of Bannerwell to lie beside a fountain and think of Tossa. I summoned her up out of nothing, her colt's grace and great sheaf of gold hair, her warm brown arms stretched wide against the sky. I dreamed her into reality, then I went with her into a world unlike our own and built a place there—built it, furnished it, plowed the soil of it and planted an orchard. I summoned Yarrel to live there, with horses and a bride for him, and Silkhands as well . . .

Only to have the world vanish when Huld came into the place and sat down beside me. "I will tell you what is in his mind," he said, hoarsely. I did not reply, only begged earnestly for him to go away, to leave me alone. He did not, only sighed deeply and began to talk.

"You have seen him. There were no Healers in Schooltown at Festival time. None. It is unimaginable that it should have been the case, but it happened. We took him away, burned as he was. I sent men in all directions to find a Healer; they found one. He was drunk, incapable. All he did was make matters worse. There was no competent Healer to be found. Days passed. The tissues died. When we found a good Healer at last, it was too late. He was as you see him . . .

"He would not believe. We have brought Healers from as far away as Morninghill, beside the Southern Sea, summoned by relays of Elators and carried here by Tragamors. None could help him appear as once he did without his Talent, his beguilement. That is still as powerful as ever. His people see him as they always have, except for a few of us, except for himself . . .

"After a time, he began to believe he could have a new body, a new face . . ."

"A new body?"

"He began to believe that, perhaps, a Healer could take another body, a healthy, unscarred body, and somehow place Mandor's mind within it."

"That's impossible."

"So they told him. Then he twisted that thought a little. He began to believe that his own body could be *changed*, into another form . . ."

"By a Shapeshifter? But, that's foolish. A Shapeshifter can only change himself, into a fustigar, perhaps,

or a nighthorse, or some other animal shape.
Shapeshifters cannot take human form other than their
own."

"Mavin is said to do so."

"*Said* to do so. And, what difference, said or real?
Does he mean to have Mavin pretend to be Mandor?
Take Mandor's shape? Move about as Mandor while
Mandor stands in his Tower room and pulls the
strings?"

"It was his intention to have me Read him, guide the
Shapeshifter in changing, guide one to take not only the
form, but also the thought . . ."

"To have you what? Read Mandor and the 'shifter at
the same time? To somehow impress one upon the other? That's evil nonsense. Where did he get such an
idea?"

"Out of desperation," said Huld. "Out of fury and
pain and refusal to die or to live as he is."

"And what would happen to Mavin, did she come?
Would she be one more Gamesman used up, lost in
play? As I would have been lost in play?"

Huld flushed, only a little. "All of us are lost sooner
or later. It has never been tried. Who is to say it would
not work."

I sneered. "If I were Mavin put to such a test, I would
try my best to shift into the form of a waddle-hog."

"She would not if she cared for you, or cared for
Mertyn. For, if she did, you would die, and Mertyn as
well, and all others whom she might hold dear." He was
hard as metal. For the first time I realized that he was
quite serious. He might not believe in it, but he intended
to do what he could to make it happen. I turned from
him, sickened. He went on as though he had not noticed. "Unfortunately, you do not know where Mavin
is, or even whether she still lives. Which means we cannot use you to find her. However, it is probable that
Mertyn knows, and we do know where he is."

I left him there, unable to bear any more of his talk, his quiet exposition of villainy, treachery, and evil. It was Talisman to King's Blood one if Mertyn did not love me, Talisman to King's Blood ten if he did. We were thalani, and I had never known it. Did he love me? Since that was the condition which would lead to the most pain and confusion, undoubtedly he did. Had Yarrel been with me, he would have accused me of cynicism. What I felt was utter despair, which was not lightened when I found a letter from Mandor on my bed. It was not long.

As Mertyn's love for you led him to protect you, so was I turned into this monster. So, let his love for you be used to turn me back again . . .
You are not Gamesman, now or ever. You are pawn, mine, to throw into the Game as I will. Mavin will come, or you will die . . .

I laughed until the tears ran down my face. So Mandor had not thought such a treacherous thing, according to Huld. By the seven hells and the hundred devils, he had done. He had thought every wickedness, every pain which could be put upon me, and he was bound by his rakshasa to bind me with each one and every one until I was dead. Well, if I were dead, they could not put anything upon me. I left the room as silently as possible, creeping through the still halls to the twisting stair which led into the Tower. The stair went past Mandor's rooms and on, up onto the parapet, twenty manheights above the rocks at the river's edge. It was all I could think of which could be done swiftly, and I prayed that someone would know I had not killed myself out of dishonor.

At Mandor's door I paused. Huld's voice was raised within, almost shouting, and I could hear it clearly. "And I tell you once more, Mandor, that he knows nothing of help to you, nothing. Do you think I would

lie to you if there were any hope? Do you not dishonor
yourself in this treacherous use of one who loved you?
You dishonor me!"

Ah, I thought, the Demon may do Mandor's will,
but he gets no joy of it. I went on, up past the little spi-
raling windows, out through the low door onto the lead
roof, covered with slates. I did not see the figure leaning
upon the parapet until I had thrown my own leg over
and was ready to leap out into waiting oblivion. By then
it was too late. I was caught in huge arms and held tightly as eyes glittered at me through winds of paint. A Seer.
His shout went up. Armsmen of one kind and another
came in answer. I was carried down the stairs to confront Huld where he stood just outside Mandor's door.

"That was foolish, lad," he said sadly.

"I thought not," I answered him. "Death is easier
than this ugliness you do."

The huge Seer behind me thrust past to kneel at
Mandor's feet. I could tell from the way he did it that he
saw Mandor as Mandor had been. Strange. One who
could see into the future could not see clearly in the
present. "My Prince," he said, "I have Seen this
boy . . ."

There was an inarticulate shout from Mandor. The
Seer reacted as though he had heard it as a question.

"Yes, my Prince. I have Seen the boy in a form other
than the one he now wears, Seen him crowned, as a
Prince . . ."

Huld turned a burning face on me, flushed red with a
great surfeit of blood. Was he angry? I could not tell.
Some emotion burned there which I could not read even
as I felt him digging in my head, deeply enough to hurt. I
cried out and he withdrew.

"There is no knowledge of it in him . . ."

"There 'ill ve," Mandor said.

"Yes, my Prince. There will be," agreed the Seer.

Mandor turned into his room, slamming the door behind him so that it raised echoes down the stair, sounds beating upon our ears like the buffeting of bat wings. Huld motioned the guards who were holding me, and they followed him down into the depths of Bannerwell, below the pleasant gardens, into the stone of the cliff itself to a place where they chained me in a room of stone. I sat stupidly, staring at the chain.

Huld said, "You will not be able to harm yourself here. A guardsman outside the door will watch you always. This place is warm and dry and you will be well fed. You will not suffer. The Seer has Seen your future, Seen you in the guise of the Prince. This means his hope is not false, not impossible. Somehow through Mavin or through your inheritance of her Talent, Mandor's hope will be brought to fruition. You understand?"

I did not say because I did not understand. It was all foolishness, stupidity.

"For your own good, I would suggest you focus your attention upon that Talent. For the good of others as well. Mandor is impatient. He will apply every encouragement he can."

I will not weary myself with telling of the next days. I did not know what passage of time it was. There was only torchlight there, and no time except the changing of the guard and the bringing of food and the emptying of the bucket into which I emptied myself. There were quiet times during which I forgot who I was, where I was, why I was. There were terrible times when Mandor came, his face unveiled, and sat looking at me, simply looking at me for what seemed hours. There were times when he spoke and I could not understand him, and he was maddened by that. There were times when he struck me, enough to cause pain, though not enough to wound me permanently.

There were times when Huld came, came to argue, remonstrate, dig into my head to see what went on in there. Little enough, the Gameslords knew. There was little enough to find. When I was let alone I made long, dreamy memories of Tossa, summoned her up beside me and made lovers' tales and poems to her. I did not think of Mertyn or of Mavin. I did not think of Himaggery or Windlow. I did not think, in fact, more than necessary to keep me alive.

There were times when the torches went out and I was left in darkness. There was one time when I refused to eat, and they brought men to hold me down while a Tragamor forced food down my throat. After that, I ate. There was the time that Mandor—no, I do not need to remember that. He had to tie me, and I do not think he got any pleasure of it.

I will not tell of that time, for it was the same over and over for a long while. Instead, I will tell of what happened at the Bright Demesne. I did not learn of it until later, but it fits the tale here, so why should it not be told:

When those who captured me turned west down the great valley, they were seen by Yarrel and Windlow from a post high on a canyon wall. When we had gone, they sought Silkhands and Chance, finding them about eventime. They did not wait on morning, but rode swiftly east toward the Bright Demesne. At first light Yarrel told them they rode hard upon the tracks of two other horses, and they knew at once it was Dazzle and Borold. The four of them together would have been no match for Dazzle and Borold in a rage, so they took pains not to ride on the heels of those who went before. They left the road and made their way slowly through the forests, arriving warily among the outlyers of the Bright Demesne a full day after Dazzle and Borold had come there. This was about at the same time that I rode on the laboring little horse over the highest pass of the Hidamans on my way to Bannerwell. Once within

Himaggery's protection, Silkhands feared no more but went to him as swiftly as she could with the tale of Dazzle's perfidy and my capture upon her lips.

I was told later that Himaggery's meeting with old Windlow was joyous, full of tender feeling and gratitude for the old man's safety, the meeting marred only by the story of my capture and of Dazzle's infamy. Dazzle had already been sent away once more by Himaggery, sent into the eastern forests on a contrived "errand" and could not now be found without great effort. As it was, they knew only that I had been seen in company with a pawner and a Demon and some others, riding westward to some unknown destination. The horses had been of the common type which are ridden by all the mountain people, so Yarrel was of no help.

They conferred at great length about finding me, discussing this possibility and that. Had I been taken for ransom? If so, by whom? Had I been taken for some other reason? If so, what? They engaged in recriminations of themselves that Dazzle had not been Read when she returned, but Himaggery had only thought to be rid of her, not where she had been in the interim.

"My fault," he said, not once but many times. "I should have realized that she would have been involved in any mischief or wickedness which she could find or create. Why did I not have the sense to examine her, to question Borold. He would not have had the wits to oppose me . . ."

Yarrel, impatient at this long delay, simply demanded help in finding me. Himself a pawn, though that was not generally known, he summoned the courage to demand that Himaggery exert the utmost effort in finding me and aiding me if that were needed. No, I have not put that right. Yarrel did not need to summon courage. He simply was courageous. I miss him greatly in these later days.

Then was the full power of the Bright Demesne as-

sembled to the service of Himaggery. I have visualized it
so many times. It happened in that great room, the audience hall, where we had first sat for our stories. Beneath
the floor the hot waters of the springs flowed in chan-
nels, making the stones mist with steam, for they had
been recently mopped for the occasion. The walls of
that room are white, mighty blocks of stone polished to
a high gloss set in curving bays, each bay lighted with tall
windows, one above the other, each bay separated from
its neighbor by a marble pillar on which vines are
carved, and little beasts and birds, the whole inlaid with
gems and gold and other precious materials so that it
glitters in the light. Six or seven manheights above, the
dome curves up in a sweep of polished white toward
the Eye, a lens set in the center of the dome. It is cut in a
way to break the light, making small rainbows move
across the floor and walls as the world tilts. At one side
are a pair of shimmering doors, and at the other is
Himaggery's seat, a simple stone chair pillowed with
bright cushions and set only high enough that he may be
seen and heard by all. On this morning he had summoned all the Seers, Demons, and Pursuivants of his
Demesne and dependencies, and with them the
Rancelmen and others whose Talent it is to seek and
find. They came into that great room, a wide circle of
them, with another circle inside that, and inside that a
third, each Gamesman seated upon a cushion, his hands
linked to those on either side, or her hands linked it may
be, for many were women. In the center were a group of
Elators. Silkhands, who had been keeping to her room
until Dazzle was gone, Chance, and Yarrel were there
a little behind Himaggery where they would not be in
the way. Beside the seat was a bronze gong in a carved
frame, and Himaggery took the striker between his
hands as he spoke to the assembled Gamesmen.

"These two, Yarrel and Silkhands, know Peter well.
Chance has known him since he was a babe. You may

take the pattern from them and then search wide. The boy was seen last some three days ago, in company with a pawner and Demon and some company of other Gamesmen, riding west down the Long Valley. Seek well, for this Demesne is honor bound to find him . . ."

He struck the gong. Under the assembly the floors shuddered as workmen below shifted gates to allow the boiling water of the springs to surge beneath the stones. It grew hot, hotter, but only for the moment. In that moment the linked Gamesmen began to seek, each tied to another, each pulling the power of the springs below him, each sending mind into the vast forests of the Hidaman Mountains, west and north, west and south, seeking, seeking. But first . . .

To Silkhands it felt as though she had been struck by some gigantic wing, monstrous yet soft. There was none of the normal Demon tickle in her head. Instead there was a feeling that her mind was taken from her and unfolded, laid out like a linen for the ironing, spread, smoothed, almost as though multiple hands stroked it to take out each wrinkle. Then it was folded up again, just as it had been, and put away.

Yarrel and Chance did not describe it so. To them the search came as water, as though a stream ran into and away from them, bearing with it all manner of thought and memory so that they were stunned and silent when it was done, unable for many moments to think who they were or why they were in that place. This was "taking the pattern" as Himaggery had said, directing his searchers to go on the trail, like fustigars on the scent. They, with the scent of me in their nostrils, went out into the world to find me.

Later no one remembered who found the first sign. It might have been a Rancelman, one used to seeking the lost, or more likely a Pursuivant who saw through Yarrel's mind the site of that canyon entrance. In the center of the audience hall sat the Elators. When a place

could be sufficiently identified to guide her there, one
would flisk out of sight, gone, directed by that linked
Talent and her own to that distant place. There she
searched, found the tracks which the Pursuivant said
must be there, saw the direction they went, looked there
for a landmark and returned. The landmark was passed
through some Demon to another Elator who went as the
first had gone, this time to the farther point.

At one point a Seer called out as a sudden Vision interrupted the slower jump, jump, jump of Elators.
"Further North," he cried, "toward the White Peaks."
Thus the search leaped forward until an Elator found
the road once more. There were false landmarks as well
as true ones. Sometimes the Elators overshot the mark
and came out in places far from the road, sometimes the
road branched and they guessed wrong. Sometimes the
picture was dim and confused as it came from one into
the minds of the others. The pace became slower. The
room became hotter. There was no lack of power, but
the bodies which used it were growing weary. Himaggery struck the gong once more, and the water-gates beneath the floor shuddered closed.

"Eat," ordered the Wizard. "Sleep. Walk in the gardens. We will meet once more in this room at dusk."

He invited Silkhands and Yarrel to join him with old
Windlow in his own rooms for the meal. Silkhands was
full of comment and chatter, as always.

"I do not understand how this is done? What Game is
this? I have not heard of this."

"No Game, Healer. We are not playing. We are
seeking a reality, a truth. We have not done it often, not
often enough to become truly practiced at it. We have
done it only in secret, not when mischief makers were
about. If you had not insisted in being always with Dazzle, you might have taken part before this time."

"But what is it? How is it done?"

"To understand, you must first understand a Heresy . . ."

"Oh, you two and your Heresies. I have yet to understand what either of you mean by Heresy. You have said nothing I have not learned or thought a thousand times . . ."

"There are eleven Talents," said Himaggery.

"Nonsense," she contradicted him. There are thousands. All in the Index, all of them. Each type of Gamesman has his own Talent."

"No, there are only eleven."

"But . . ."

"You have asked, now be still and let me say. There are only eleven, Silkhands, twelve if you count the Immutables."

"The Immutables have no Talent!"

"Indeed? They have the power to mute our Talents, to be themselves unchanged no matter what we attempt to do. Is that not a Talent?"

"But, that's not what we mean when we say Talent . . ."

"No. But it is what is true. It is in Windlow's book."

"The Index lists thousands. I have learned their names, their dress, their types, how they move, their Demesnes, all . . ."

He turned from her to the mists and the fruit trees which mingled outside his windows. "Healer, your Talent is one of the eleven. You can name the others if you would. They are those which you have recently learned at Windlow's House."

"You mean what Windlow said about the First Eleven, from the religious books? What has that to do with . . ."

He laughed. "Silkhands, you are such a child. Do you know that elsewhere in this world there is a group of very powerful Wizards who are known, collectively, as the Council? Did you know that they have taken upon themselves to assure that there are no heretics in our world? None who speak of arrangements not found in the Index? None who talk of the Immutables having Talent? You are so innocent. Here, we can talk of it. Here you are safe, in the Bright Demesne. But you will not thank me for it.

"It was Windlow who saw it, long years ago, and taught it to me, quietly, so that it should not come to the attention of the Guardians, those of the Council whose interest it is to maintain things always as they are. It was Windlow who saw that the books of religion are actually books of history, that what was said about the descent of our forebears was indeed true.

"We are told of Didir, a Demon. Imagine, Silkhands, imagine Yarrel, a world in which there were no Talents. It will be easy for you, Yarrel. Imagine a world all pawns. No power but the power of muscle and voice, persuasion and blows, nothing else. Perhaps some power of intelligence, too. Windlow and I argue about that."

"There would be intelligence," said Yarrel. "There is power in intelligence. I know. I can imagine your world."

"Very well. Then, imagine that into this world is born one woman who can read the thoughts of others. Didir. Why is it that we call them Demons? Those who read thoughts? Hmmm? We speak of evil godlets as demons, wicked spirits are demons. Why, then, is a Reader a Demon?"

"Because they would have considered her an evil spirit, an evil force," said Yarrel. "They could not have helped but feel that way. It would have been terrible for them to have their thoughts wrenched out into the open, laid before others . . ."

"Ah, yes. Even so. And the books of religion go on. They say that one was born named Tamor, an Armiger.

The oldest books say Ayrman. Why is that do you suppose?"

"Because he could fly," said Silkhands. "Armigers can fly."

"And what would the world of pawns think of that?"

"They would wonder at him," said Yarrel. "And fear him, and perhaps hate him. I wonder that they did not kill him."

"Windlow says not," Himaggery went on. Old Windlow nodded where he sat. "Windlow says that *they*, the pawns of that world took Tamor and Didir to some other place, away from the world of the pawn."

"What other place?" said Silkhands. "What place is there?"

Himaggery shook his head. "Who knows? But Windlow believes this because he says it makes sense out of much he has read. He says that Didir and Tamor were sent away, and that thereafter they mated with one another, and either they or their offspring mated with some of the pawns who went with them. From their mating came Hafnor, an Elator. The Talent of an Elator is to transport himself, or herself, from place to place. Generations later, from the family and lineage of Didir came the first Seer, Sorah. And so forth. And when you have listed them all, you have eleven."

"But there *are* more. There are Heralds, and Witches, and Rancelmen, and . . ."

"The Witch has three of the eleven," said Himaggery, patiently. "Firemaking, beguilement, and the power to store power, as Sorcerers do. A Witch has none of these in the strength that those who hold them singly do, but the witch has all three."

"And Heralds?"

"Heralds have the power of flight, but only in small, and the power of Seeing, also in small, and a slight ability to move things with their minds, as Tragamors do."

"And Rancelmen?"

"Seeing, Reading the thoughts of others, both in small, and a natural curiosity which seems to have little to do with Talent."

Yarrel said slowly, "Reading, Seeing, Flying, Transporting, Moving, Storing, Healing, Firemaking, then—what would you call it?"

"Beguilement, the power of Kings and Princes. A power to make others believe in one, follow one. Sometimes the Talent is called 'follow-me.' And this leaves two more: Shapeshifting and Necromancy. Those are the eleven. There are no others, except for the one held by the Immutables."

"Which the books of religion say was created purposefully by two Wizards, Barish and Vulpas." Yarrel was very thoughtful. "I can imagine why they did it. They probably saw all the people without Talents being eaten up in the Game, and they felt it was wrong. So, they created a power which would protect the pawns from harm, and they gave it away. But only to some," he concluded bitterly.

"Perhaps there was not time to give it to all," Silkhands said.

"Perhaps they were prevented from doing so," said Windlow. "When first I read of that act, I wondered why two Wizards would behave so. Then, at last, I knew. A Wizard would do such a thing when he learned the word *Justice*. It is a very old word. It is in my book. It means to do what is right, to correct what is wrong, to find the correct way."

"Correct?" asked Silkhands. "I do not understand correct."

"No, we do not know the word," Himaggery agreed. "In the Game it is only the rules which matter. The rules are always broken, and there are few penalties for that, but it is still the rules which matter. Few care for what is honorable. None cares for what is right or just. They care only for the rules. Windlow says the rules were cre-

ated to bring some order out of chaos, but over the centuries the rules became more important than anything
else. They became the end rather than the means. Now,
I have taught you heresy. There are those in the world
who wish the Game to continue as it has been played for
generation upon generation. There are those who do
not care for the idea of justice—and well they might not.
Thus far we have been fortunate, the Bright Demesne
has been fortunate. We have not been challenged in a
Great Game. We have made common fortune with
some few Immutables and spoken with them from time
to time on neutral ground. Much do they suspect us,
however. We hold a tenuous peace. It cannot last forever, and it may be that Peter's abduction is the falling
pebble which starts the avalanche.

"Windlow Sees, and he tells me to have good heart. I
trust him with my life and love him with my soul, as
though we were thalani. But I am not courageous always," confessed Himaggery. "I have not that Talent."

"Lord," asked Silkhands, "what Talent do you have?
What is the Talent of Wizards?"

He laughed at her and rumpled her hair but did not
answer. "If I have any, it is to link Gamesmen together
to pursue this word, this justice. If I have any at all, it is
that."

9

Shapeshifter

The assembled Talents of the Bright Demesne went at it
again at dusk, and again on the morning following.
By noon of the second day they had tracked me to
Bannerwell, and one Seer at least told them I was alive
within its walls. It took them a day or two to send a Pursuivant to a place nearby, for though Pursuivants have
the power of transporting themselves, as Elators do, it is
not as potent a Talent. They have the power of Reading,
as Demons do, as well, but again it is not as intense.
Thus, my friends were not really surprised when the
Pursuivant returned to say he could pick up thoughts
which he believed were mine, but he could not be sure.
He had, however, picked up a clear reference to Mertyn
from several sources in and around Bannerwell, and this
was enough to make some in the assembly turn their attention toward Mertyn's House in Schooltown.

From that moment it was not long until they discovered my parentage—or should it be motherage.
Strange, I had not thought of that before. I knew that
Talents were inherited, that they might be traced both
from the female and male parent, but even when I had
heard that I was Mavin's son, I had had no curiosity
about my father. It was, even when I thought of it, only
a passing thought, and that was much later. As soon as
Himaggery was told of it, he sent an Elator to Mertyn,

begging him to travel to the Bright Demesne. He broke the rules in doing so. Elators do not, by the rules, carry messages from one Demesne to another. That is left to Heralds or, on occasion, Ambassadors. Though none of us knew it, it was fortunate Himaggery held the rules so in contempt. Mandor's own Heralds were even then on the road to Schooltown.

They arrived to find Mertyn gone. He had taken a swift ship from Schooltown to sail across the Gathered Waters and down the Middle River to Lake Yost. He had not left word with any in Mertyn's House where he had gone. Himaggery's Elator, who had set Mertyn on the road, offered no help to Mandor's Heralds, who had no choice but to take lodging in Schooltown and await Mertyn's return. Eventually they gave up and returned to Bannerwell to face Mandor's wrath. The day they returned was a day I do not wish to remember.

Meantime, each day Himaggery would seek out Windlow, who sat in his pleasant rooms over the garden reading my book, to ask him what should be done next. The old man would close his wrinkly eyes and lean back against the side of the window, the sun falling sweetly on his face in quiet warmth, the mists drifting up and away as they always did, and invoke a long silence during which he searched for Seeings. Then at last he would open his eyes and say what he could.

On one day it was, "Peter is not in immediate danger, Himaggery. However, he is desperate, and very lonely, and without hope."

Silkhands was in the room. She said at once, "We must go to him. Now. While the rest of you figure out what it is you will do . . ." Himaggery began to object, but was interrupted by the old man.

"No. Don't forbid her, Himaggery. That may be a very good idea. Healers are generally respected, almost always safe. If she goes with Yarrel and Chance—a Healer riding with two servants? Can you pretend to be servants?'' He asked it of Yarrel, knowing Yarrel's pride.

"I can't pretend," said Yarrel. "I can be." And he bowed before Silkhands as though he were her groom. "If Silkhands will learn her part."

"Oh, I will do," she pledged.

So, the three of them set out for Bannerwell, not over the high passes of the Hidamans, as I had come there, but up the western side of Middle River and then along the foothills west in the valley of the Banner itself. Before they left, Himaggery took Yarrel aside and told him of other Seeings which Windlow had had recently.

"There is to be a Grand Demesne, lad. A great Game. Silkhands must not know of it, for they will Read her in Bannerwell. They will not bother you or Chance. Pawns are not considered in such matters. But you must know, in order to plan . . ."

While those three left the Bright Demesne, Himaggery plotted and plotted again, and Mertyn sailed toward him, and Mandor raged, and I sat in the rocky cell and dreamed myself elsewhere or hoped I could die. All of us were thinking of me. No one was thinking of Dazzle.

She, however, returned from her errand to learn that Silkhands had come and gone, which threw Dazzle into a compelling fury. She was full of wrath, full of vengeance against all those she fancied had wronged her, with Borold offering a willing ear to all her fancies. Thus, in a quiet dark hour, Dazzle and Borold rode out on Silkhands' trail. Perhaps they had murder in mind. Perhaps she feared what Himaggery would do if Silkhands were hurt directly and so plotted some more indirect revenge. No one knows now what she thought then, save only that she meant Silkhands no good.

Time passed. I knew none of this. I knew nothing save my own continuing sorrow and despair.

Then, one time I was sitting on the cot in the cell where they chained me, the room dim and shadowed from the torch which burned smokily in the corridor outside the grilled door; the guard who stood there half nodding, catching himself, then nodding again; the place silent as the moon, when there was a flicker of movement at the edge of my eye. There was only stone there, nothing could have moved, so I turned my head, surprised, to see an Elator framed for an instant against the rock. He gave me one sharp look and was gone. I thought I had imagined it, had imagined the slim form in its tight wash-leather garb, close-hooded, appearing almost naked in silhouette. But, could I have imagined that furtive, hasty glare? The matter was resolved at once, for the guardsman shouted and ran away down the hall. He had seen it, too.

They came then, Huld and Mandor, Huld to trample through my mind with heavy feet, scuffing and scraping, trying to find what was not there once more, Mandor to rail and spit and rage, his horrible face made more hideous still in wrath. I choked and was silent and let them do it. What else could I do? Each time it happened, I was amazed anew that the guards did not see Mandor as I did. I knew from their conversation that none in Bannerwell saw him as I did except Huld. To them all he was still the shining Prince, the elegant Lord. I had one guard tell me that he envied me, *me,* for it was said abroad that the Prince had loved me.

"He does not know," Huld told Mandor for perhaps the thousandth time. "There may have been an Elator, but Peter does not know him or whence he came or for what reason."

There was an inarticulate shout from Mandor which Huld seemed to understand perfectly. "No, Mandor, I cannot be mistaken. If someone searches for the boy, then he does so—or *she* does so without the boy's knowledge. How should he know? How long have you kept him like this? Who would have informed him of anything? Surely you do not think he has become a Seer. Let our preparations for Great Game go forward! I doubt not we will be challenged, and soon, but let the boy alone!"

There was another slather of spitting words. Mandor's attempts at speech sounded to me like fighting tree cats, all yowls and hissing. Huld replied again, "It is possible that Mertyn searches for him, possible that Mavin searches for him, possible even that the High King searches for him, if we are to believe that Witch we brought with us from the High Demesne. All that is possible. But it is *certain,* your Seers tell us, that someone has started a Great Game and Bannerwell is being moved upon. What then? Direct me. I am your thalan and your servant."

"Get Divulger," said Mandor. Once in a great while his words were very clear, and this was one of those times. "Get Divulger."

Huld shouted. "He cannot tell you if he does not know, not even under torture."

"He can shif'," said Mandor, stalking away down the echoing corridor. "Shif' or die."

Huld said nothing, swallowed. Bared his teeth as though in a snarl, but it was not at me. At length, he said, "This is not honorable, Peter. I would not command it were I not commanded to do so. He orders you put to torture in the vain hope that pain will force Talent to come forth, if there is any to come forth. Some say that Talents emerge when needed to save us. I do not know if that is true. I beg your pardon . . ."

And he left me. Vain wish, I thought, oh Huld who has no honor. Vain wish if you will do as you are bid no matter what you are bid. My mind was afire, thinking up and discarding a hundred schemes. What might I do? What might I say? I did not want to meet torture, knowing as I did what it meant. I had seen much from my rocky cell, more than needful, for the torture dungeons lay below and men had been dragged to and fro before my eyes. I thought of Mertyn, of Himaggery, wondered if they would send help, knew it would come too late. I thought of Chance and Yarrel, wished they could comfort me. I thought of old Windlow, Windlow and his birds and his herbs . . . and remembered. Windlow's herbs. I had still in my pocket leaves of that herb he had given us in the canyons, that herb which had let us leave our bodies to become as grass.

I tugged out the scrap of cloth, heard men coming, fumbled the leaves out and into my mouth, returning a few to my pocket. If I could keep my head and there were a few moments of peace, perhaps I could separate myself from my body enough not to feel pain. Footsteps approached. The Divulger peered in through the grill, a hairy man, arms bare to the shoulder, black hood across his eyes. leather-shirted with high boots.

"Come out," he said, and I came, following him like a lamb, like a lamb. We passed the guard. We were alone. He at my side, face set in contempt. He of the hard body, heavy body, muscular arms, hairy neck, slope of shoulder, flat skull, small eyes peering through the half hood, heavy, the feet slap, slap, slap, the feel of the soles as they hit the stone, the curve of a toenail biting into the flesh with a sullen pain, the broken skin on the knuckle of the right hand, memory of the taste of morning grain furring the square, yellow teeth, running my tongue across them to feel the broken one where a victim had lashed out with a stone in his hand, not like this boy, only a baby, wouldn't last a minute on the rack, would come to pieces like a stewed fowl . . . and turned to look at the victim to see himself as in a mirror, himself looming hugely in the corridor, to feel the torch crash down across his brow, the metal band crushing out thought, life. Then there was only one of us in the corridor alive, and one of us dead, and both of us the same, the same.

It was not until I saw my hand holding the snatched up torch that I realized something had happened; not until I turned to see my face reflected in the metal plate over a cell peek-hole that I knew what had happened. It was true. I had a Talent. I had inherited from Mavin Manyshaped who was said to take human form other than her own. Oh, yes. Indeed. As I had done.

And not only the form. For there, open to me as though in a book, were all the memories of that morning, the man's own name, faces of those he knew, bits and pieces of the fortress laid out as though on a map. I tried to remember something further back, his childhood, his parents, but there was nothing there. No. Only a few, loose thoughts, a sufficient baggage to carry about for a few hours, names, places, faces, and one's own job. I had been thinking of that with anticipation, I the Divulger. I, Peter, was only frightened by it. What now? We two still occupied the corridor, one alive, one dead.

Well, I would be safe so long as they thought me the Divulger, one Grimpt by name. Thus, they must not find the other one, the original Grimpt. I caught the body beneath the arms and tugged it along the corridor. The memories which I had taken over with the body were enough to guide me. The torture dungeon lay this way, and in it were pits, oubliettes, places where bodies might be hidden for a time or lost forever. Before I disposed of him, however, I took inventory of my own form because something was not . . . ah, my clothing. I had taken the Grimpt form well enough, but not the form of the clothing. My own rags still hung on me, the trousers ripped at the seams by a sudden excess of flesh. I peeled them off and stripped him to put his clothes on me over my shirt. Never mind the stains of blood. There were others, older, dried to crusts of brown. That, seemingly, was part of the costume. I remember the herb which Windlow had given me. There was a little of it left, not much. Perhaps enough to make another shift, I thought, and then it might not be needed after that.

Come to, I encouraged myself. There will be time enough to think of such things later. Now it is time to assure safety. So, dead Grimpt went down the oubliette. Live Grimpt went back up the corridor to a place where he might call to the Guardsman outside Peter's cell door.

"Hey. You there, what's yer name, Bossle is it? Well, run on up t'the kitchen and bring us a mug. I'll put what's left of this'un back to bed. G'won now, it's thirsty work enough." The man was only a common guardsman in a rust-splotched hauberk with little more Talent than a pawn, a Flugleman perhaps. He opened his mouth to argue, decided against it, leaned his weapon against the wall and went clattering up the stairs. I moved to the open cell, went in, curled the thin mattress beneath the blanket as though someone lay there, put Peter's shoes beside the cot and his trousers under the blanket, showing a little at the edge, came out of the place and locked it. I met the guardsman at the foot of the stairs, gave him the key, told him a filthy story which I found in Grimpt's mind ready to be recounted, drank the beer, slapped him heavily upon his back and went up the stairs whistling tunelessly.

Huld was waiting for me at the top of the stairs. Grimpt's mind said "bow," so I bowed.

"Well?" he asked.

I shrugged. "He didn't say nothing . . . except what they all say," I sniggered. Huld made an expression of distaste which I feigned not to notice. "I put 'im away. Y'wan it done again today?" The question was automatic, requiring no thought.

"No." He shuddered. "No." He turned and left me,

the expression of distaste more pronounced as though he smelled something. I, too, smelled something, and realized that it was the smell of a Divulger's clothing—old blood, and smoke, and sweat. Grimpt had a place, a place with a door on it, a filthy place. I went there. Once inside with the door locked behind me, I spent some time in thought.

When they discovered that Peter was gone, they would question the guard. He would know nothing, but he would turn attention to Grimpt. Then they would question Grimpt. My surface thoughts were Grimpt's, well enough, but they held recent memories which would not stand up to examination. No. I could not remain Grimpt. It would be necessary to become something else, take some other form—something unimportant, beneath notice. I left the filthy little cubby and wandered out toward the courtyard, full of the tumult of men hauling the sections of the Great Game ovens onto the paving stones, the screech and clangor of hammers and wheels, the rumbling rush of wagons crossing the bridge bringing wood for the ovens. The bridge was down, the gate up to allow the wagons to move in and out, but each crew was guarded and there were more guards at the bridge. It would not be easy to leave the fortress, so much was clear. A Divulger would have no reason to go into the forest; any attempt to do so would cause suspicion.

The lounging guardsmen were all alert, scanning the high dike to the east through which the Banner flowed. They had been told to expect challenge or attack and were keyed up by recent admonitions from their leaders. One man was much preoccupied with the pain of a sore foot. From inside an iron gate came a gardener's thoughts, mixed irritation and anger that the help he had been promised had not come. It was a natural thing, so natural that long moments passed before I realized what was happening. Grimpt was able to *Read*.

I tried to find something more in the minds of the guardsmen or the gardener, but could not. Seemingly, the Talent was a small one, able to pick up only surface thoughts. Quite enough for a torturer, I thought. The thoughts of his victims were probably very much surface thoughts. What else could a Divulger do? The question brought its own answer as a gate swung toward my hand. Yes, of course. The Divulger would be able to Move things, slightly. I tried to lift a paving stone and felt only a dull ache. No, this too was a small Talent. Well, it was one which might be helpful.

The gardener was a pawn, he had no Talent. He was a little angry, but unsuspicious. So, let the man have the help he had been promised. Let the gardener have his boy. I slipped into a niche of the wall where it extended out over the moat into a privy used by the servants of the courtyard, and the grooms. No one had noticed me. The guardsmen had begun a straggling procession toward the kitchens; the remaining ones were looking away toward the hills. I took one leaf of the herb, only one, and bit down on it as I thought about a boy, a vacant-eyed boy, a boy dressed only in a dirty shirt, a brown-legged boy with greasy, brownish hair and no-colored eyes, an unremarkable boy with a gap in his teeth. I thought of the boy, the boy, how he would feel about helping the gardener, harder work than he liked, but they told him to help or no food, so he'd help, damn them all anyways.

The boy put Grimpt's boots and clothing down the privy, belted Peter's shirt tightly around his slim waist and stepped out of the privy and into the garden where he stood sullenly at the gardener's elbow.

"They told me off to help you," he said.

"Oh, they did, did they? Well, it's about time. Promised me help this morning, they did, and not a sign of it. You take that barrow, there, and go fill it up at the dung heap. Dig down good, now, you understand. I don't want any fresh. I want old stuff that's all rotten down.

And be quick about it." As the boy turned away, the man asked, "And what's your name?"

"What's it matter?" the boy muttered.

"What's it matter? Well, it don't matter. But I got to call you something, don't I? Can't go around yelling 'boy' or I'd have half the young ones in the place buggering around. I need something to lay a tongue to . . ."

"Name's Swallow," the boy said. "Y'can call me Swall; they mostly do."

10

Swallow

Swallow had a dirty face and could spit through the gap in his teeth. There had been a boy once at Mertyn's House who could do that; Peter had envied him. Swallow had lice in his hair, or at least he scratched as though he did, and an evil, empty-headed leer. When the gardener received a noon meal, Swallow received one as well, a large bowl of meat and grain and root vegetables, the same again at night with the addition of a mug of bitter beer and a lump of cheese the size of his fist.

The gardener had a hut beside the fortress wall, near the kitchen gardens. The cooks had a place near the kitchen. Others had cubbies and corners here and there, closets and niches hidden in the thick walls behind tapestries. Swallow found a place in the hay loft above the stables, a good enough place, both warm and dry. He was to every intent and eye invisible. No one in the place noticed him, and no one in the place except the gardener could have said who he was or how long he had been there. Swallow was one of them, the pawns, the unconsidered. When, in the middle of the afternoon, there was a great tumult in the castle with men running to and fro and a confused trumpeting of voices as a search for Grimpt was conducted, no one thought of Swallow. No one spoke to him, or asked him anything. Swallow watched them running about, his mouth hanging open and his face vacant, but they did not see him.

141

All night long while Swallow slept burrowed deep in the warm hay, the castle hummed with men coming and going, wagons rumbling toward and away from the sound of axes in the forest. He may have wakened briefly at the noise, but went to sleep at once again. Swallow had worked hard all day. What was this confusion to him?

Thus he could be completely surprised the next morning when he listened to the whispers of the guardsmen as they ate their first meal in the early sunlight of the yard.

"The Prisoner is gone, they say. Gone right out of his clothes. Nothing left of him at all."

"And Grimpt gone, too? Filthy sot. I'll believe that when bunwits lay eggs."

"No. It's true. He's gone right enough. They've searched every corner for him. It's said now he went down the privy and over the moat."

"Down the privy. Ay. That's the place for old Grimpt, right enough."

"They found his boots in the moat. Fished them out."

"What's it all about? Do they say Grimpt took the prisoner with him?"

"No. There's talk of a Great Game coming. The prisoner was taken out by Powers, by a Wizard, they say. Or burned up in his clothes by a Firedrake."

"The clothes 'ud burn, too."

"They say not."

"Ah, well. They'll say anything."

The gardener had been listening also, came to himself and shut his mouth with an audible snap, caught Swallow by an arm and spun him around. "Enough of this loll-bagging about. Great Game or no, there's lawn to level, and we'd best at it."

Swallow spent the better part of the day rolling a heavy cylinder of stone over clipped grass, muttering the whole time to anyone within ear shot. The gardener wasn't listening, but Swallow let no opportunity for complaint pass by. Huld came through the garden at noon, his face drawn and tired. He did not notice the boy. Swallow saw Huld but kept his eyes resolutely upon the stone roller. It was not his business to draw the attention of Demons. Mandor, too, came into the garden, but by that time Swallow was having his lunch in the courtyard, almost out of sight around the corner of the iron gate. Mandor saw nothing. His eyes were fixed and glazed, and there was dried foam upon the corners of his mouth. Swallow looked up from his bowl to see adoration upon the faces around him. His own face became adoring at once, and he did not start eating again until those around him did so.

Late in the afternoon two Armigers rode in, bringing with them two pawns and a Healer. Swallow watched them ride in, as did everyone else in the place, his mouth open, his fingers busy scratching himself. The Healer was escorted into the castle, and the pawns were told to stand by the wall until they were summoned. It seemed to Swallow that they looked almost familiar, and he turned away to continue his work as Peter said to him softly, "Swallow, that is my friend Yarrel and my friend Chance." Hearing the voice from within frightened Swallow, and it was a long moment before Peter could fight his way to the surface again.

"There is more to this business than I thought," I said to myself. I had created a reality, a half-person who grew more real with each passing hour, more real than myself. And yet, to be safe, it had to be so. Swallow had to be more real than Peter, without any thoughts which would attract attention. I sank below the surface of me, thinking of myself as a fish.

Fish, fish. I could set a hook into this fish, a hook which would pull it up to the surface when it was needed but would let it swim down into the darkness otherwise. A hook. The faces of my friends, the names of Mertyn and Himaggery and Windlow. These would be my looks. When these pulled, I would rise to peek above the water only to sink again quickly out of sight. I imagined the hook, barbed, silver, tough as steel. I set it deep into Peter and let him go.

Along toward evening a very beautiful woman and a Herald rode into Bannerwell escorted by guardsmen. Swallow saw them, though they did not see Swallow. The beautiful woman demanded an audience with Prince Mandor, and she spoke of Silkhands. The hook set and Peter rose. I said to Swallow, "When night falls, get up into those vines along the side of the hall and find a window." Then I went away again. Swallow listened. He heard me, but showed no signs of having done so. He went on his gap-toothed way, spitting and scratching and slobbering over his food as though the evening bowl had been the last he would ever receive, then off to his hay loft to fall into empty sleep.

When the moon had risen, and the place was quiet except for the pacing of the guardsmen upon the battlements, Swallow woke and sneaked through black shadow into the vines on the castle wall, century old vines with trunks thick as his body. He was hidden within them as he climbed, empty-headed, high above the paved courtyard into a night land of roofs and across silvered slates to a high window which looked down into the great hall. He picked out pieces of bent lead to make a gap in that window larger, pulling out fragments of glass, softly, softly, a thief in the night. Then he could see and hear what went on below.

Silkhands was there, and Peter rose to that hook, fished up out of liquid darkness to watch and listen.

"I have come, Prince Mandor, because the Wizard Himaggery has traced a young friend of his here, Peter, former student of King Mertyn at Mertyn's House. You knew him there." It was not precisely a question. I heard Mandor's gargle and wondered how Silkhands understood it. Then I found that if I listened, without looking at him, letting the sound enter my ears without judging it, I, too could almost understand it. Almost it was the voice of someone I had once cared for . . . But Silkhands went on, "The Wizard, Himaggery, believes that the boy may not have come to Bannerwell of his own will. He sends me to ascertain whether he is well."

"Oh, he is well. Quite well. He is not here just now, gone off for a day or two on a hunting expedition. He'll undoubtedly be back within a few days. You are welcome to wait for him, Healer. You need not worry about Peter. He's well taken care of."

If Silkhands had spoken with the Elator who saw me in the dungeons, she knew Mandor lied. If she had spoken with that Elator then she would not have come to Bannerwell with this transparent story, for she would know that Mandor's Demons would Read her. No. She knew I was in Bannerwell, but she did not know under what conditions. She did not know exactly where I was, or she would not have dared come to ask for me in such innocence.

Another voice floated up to the high window from which I watched, silvery sweet and deadly. "Oh, Sister, why do you tell such lies? You know that you were not sent for any such reason. The Wizard cares nothing for the boy, nothing. If he has sent you, it is for some treacherous purpose of his own."

It was Dazzle. I peered down to see her standing against a tapestry, posed there like a statue. Her pose was almost exactly the one which Mandor had assumed when I first saw him in his rooms, profile limned against a background, pale, graceful hands displayed to advantage. Mandor was regarding her with fixed attention. Silkhands had become as still as some small wild thing, surprised too much by a predator to move. When she spoke, her voice was tight with strain.

"The Wizard cares much for Peter, Dazzle. As he has cared for you, and for Borold, and for all who have

come to the Bright Demesne. The Prince needs only
have his Gamesmen Read my thought to know I do not
lie . . ."

"Or to know you have found some way to hide a lie,
Sister. I am of the opinion that the Wizard is clever
enough to have found such a way. He is very clever, and
ambitious . . ." She cast a lingering look at Mandor,
turning away from him so that the look came over her
shoulder. It was all pose, pose, pose, each posture more
perfect than the last. Only I could see the horror of her
skull's head, her ravaged features confronting that other
skull's head across the room. Mandor did not see. Dazzle did not see. Oh, Gamelords, I thought, they are
using beguilement on one another, and neither sees
what is there. She went on in that voice of poisonous
sweetness, "Borold will bear me out. He, too, is of the
same opinion." As, of course, he was. Borold had no
opinion Dazzle had not given him.

"Well," Mandor said, his voice cold and hard, "Time
will undoubtedly make all plain. Until then, you will be
my guest, Healer. And you, Priestess. Both. If there is
some Game at large in the countryside, we would not
want to risk your lovely lives by letting you leave these
protecting walls untimely."

From the height I saw Silkhands shiver. Dazzle only
preened, posed, ran long fingers through her hair. "As
you will, Prince Mandor. I appreciate such hospitality,
as would anyone who had come for any honest reason . . ."

Mandor gestured to servants who led them both
away, each in a different direction. I watched the way
Silkhands went. I might need to find her later.

Then Mandor was joined by Huld, and the two of
them spoke together while I still listened.

"Have the guardsmen found Divulger? Any sign of
him?"

"Only the boots in the moat, Lord. There is no

discernible reason he should have made off with the boy."

"Oh, don't be a fool, Huld. He didn't make off with the boy. He killed the boy. That's why he fled, in fear of his life."

"We've found no body."

"When the moat is drained, the body may appear. Or, he may have hidden it deep, Huld, in the Caves of Bannerwell. If you wanted to hide a body, or yourself, what better place than the tombs and catacombs of Bannerwell. Things lost there may never be found again . . ."

I sneaked away across the slates, summoning Swallow back and telling him to do this and that and then another thing. Which he did. He went to the kitchens and sat about within hearing of the cooks and stewards until one entered the place saying that the Healer in the corner rooms on the third floor had had no evening meal and needed food. There was tsking from the cooks, kind words about Healers in general, and vying between two sufferers as to which of them should take the meal to her when it was ready. Enough.

The two pawns who had come with her were still in the courtyard, crouched along the wall. Swallow slouched toward them, spoke to the guard nearby. "They c'n sleep in the stable hay along of me if they'd mind to . . ." The guard ignored him. He had not been told to watch these two inconsiderable creatures. Swallow kicked at Chance's boots. "Softer there than here, and you c'n bring your things."

The two rose and followed him to the loft to lay themselves wearily down, with many grunts and sighs. Swallow sat in the dark away from them, letting the sight of their faces fish Peter up out of the dark waters to whisper, "Yarrel. Yarrel, listen to me. It's Peter."

He sat up, staring wildly about. "Peter? Where are you?"

"Shhh. I am here in the shadow."

"Come out here, into the moonlight. We expected to find you in the dungeons." I did not move, and he said warily, "Is this some trickery?"

I was very tired. I did not want to use any more of Windlow's herb, there was so little left. At that moment I could not remember the "how" of changing back, and I was too tired to try. Instead I said, "No trick, Yarrel. Listen, you and I stood on the parapet of Mertyn's House and saw a Demon and two Tragamors riding to Festival. You said the horses came from Bannerwell, remember? You said it to me. No one would know of that but us."

"A Demon might have Read it," he said coldly.

"Oh, a Demon might, but wouldn't. Think of something to ask me, then . . ."

"I ask you one thing only. Come into the light!"

Sighing, I moved forward. He seized me roughly by the shoulder and shook me. "You. You are not Peter."

It was Chance who said, "Yarrel. Look at his eyes, his face. This is Peter right enough." Evidently even in my weariness, I had let my own form come forward a little, my own face. Still, Chance had been very quick. I wondered at that moment whether he had not known all along who my mother was, whether he had not perhaps expected something of the kind. The thought was driven away by Yarrel's chilly, hostile voice.

"Shifter. You're a Shifter."

I slumped down, head on knees. He who had been my friend for so long was now so unfriendly. "I am the son of Mavin Manyshaped," I confessed. "She is full sister to Mertyn. I was told this by Huld, thalan to Mandor, as Mertyn is to me. He Read it in Mertyn's mind at Festival time." There were tears running down my legs, tears from tiredness. "Oh, Yarrel, I would rather have been a pawn in a quiet place, but that isn't what I am . . ."

Chance reached forward to stroke my arm, and I intercepted a stern look he directed at Yarrel. "Well, lad, if there has to be a Talent, why not a biggun, that's what I say. If you're going to make a noise, might as well make it with a trumpet as with a pot-lid, right?''

Yarrel had moved away from us, spoke now from some distance in that same cold voice. "Pot-lid or trumpet, Chance, but a Shifter, still. Shifty in one, shifty in all, or so I have always learned. Not Peter any more, at least. I am certain of that.''

"That's not the way it is," I screamed at him in an ago-nized whisper. "You don't understand *anything*!" I knew this was a mistake as soon as I had said it, for his voice was even more hostile when he answered.

"Perhaps you will enlighten us. Perhaps you will tell us 'how it is,' and what you intend to do . . .''

"I don't know," I hissed. "If I knew what to do, I'd have done it by now. I know I have to get Silkhands and you two out of this place, somehow. Mandor is mad and if he can use her in any way to do evil against those he imagines are his enemies, he will do so. And Dazzle is here to make sure he imagines enemies. He could easily give Silkhands to the Divulgers, as he did me . . .''

But it was not Yarrel who calmed me and comforted me and told me all that I have recounted about Himaggery's Demesne and the surety of a Great Game building around Bannerwell. No, it was Chance, com-fortable Chance, dependable Chance. Only when I spoke of Mandor's wild plan to link some various Talents together to get himself a new body did Yarrel speak, saying roughly, "More minds than one on that idea. Himaggery works along that line as well, to link the Talents of the Bright Demesne. In Himaggery's hands it might not go ill for my people, but in Man-dor's . . .''

"Himaggery marches against Mandor for your sake, Peter," said Chance. "What will you do?''

"I hoped you would help me. I don't know what to do next. I don't really understand how this Shifting works.

I've only done it twice. The first time it just happened, not even intended. I thought you and Yarrel . . ."

Yarrel interrupted, firmly, coldly. "The Talent is yours. I will not take responsibility for it. It is yours by birth, yours by rearing. We are no longer schoolfellows to plot together. You have gone beyond that . . ."

"But, Yarrel . . ." I stopped. I didn't know what to say to him. This chance was unexpected, sudden. I remembered his saying to me on the way to the High Demesne that I might gain a Talent which would make us un-friends, but surely he would not pre-judge me in this fashion. Except that . . . it had been a Shapeshifter who had done great harm to his family. Except that. Oh, Yarrel.

Chance said, "We're as good as rat's meat if Mandor knows who we are, lad. From what you say, Silkhands should be out and away from here as soon as may be. If this Talent of yours can help us, time it did so, I'd say. Great Game is coming. It would be better not to be caught in the middle of it."

"A Great Game," I said miserably. I turned away from them to lie curled on my side, hurt at Yarrel's coldness. After a time, I slept. I dreamed of a Grand Demesne, a Great Game gathering around Bannerwell. The ovens in the courtyard were red hot, their mouths gaping like monstrous mouths came to eat the people of Bannerwell. Stokers labored beside them, black against the flame. Once more I saw the flicker of Shifters in and out of the press of battle, Elators in and out of the lines of Armigers upon the battlements, saw fire raining from the sky, a sky full of Dragons and Firedrakes and enormous forms I had not seen before. And there, far at the edge of vision, gathered at the forest edges, were the pawns with their hayforks and scythes, stones in their hands. I woke sweating, gasping for air. The dark hours were upon the place. I rose wearily and went from the stables through the garden down to the little orchard which grew behind low walls over the abrupt fall to the River.

I needed someone with more knowledge than I had. If I found someone, however, what would I do? Kill him for whatever thoughts were on the surface of his brain? Likely they would be only about his dinner or his mistress or his gout, and I'd be no better off. I needed to know what I could do and had no idea how to begin. So, there in the darkness among the trees I tried to use my Talent.

After a time, it was no longer difficult. I found I could become anything I could invent or visualize, any number of empty-headed creatures like Swallow, male or female, though there were things about the female form which were uncertain at best. I could turn myself back into Grimpt, or into something else which didn't look or smell like Grimpt but had Grimpt's small Talents. The kitchen cat meauwed at me from the orchard grass, and I laid my hands on it to try to take that shape, only to burst out of the attempt with heart pounding in a wild panic. The cat's brain was so small. As soon as I began to be in it, it began to close in from all sides, pressing me smaller and smaller to crush me. Was it only that it was small? Let others find out. I would not try a creature that size again.

By the time I heard the cock gargling at the false dawn from atop the dung heap, I knew why it was that Shifters were said not to take human form. Had it not been for the panic, Windlow's herb, and my own inheritance, I would not have been able to do so when I changed to Grimpt. Only ignorance had let me make up the person of Swallow. In the dark hours I had learned that I could change only if the pattern were there, only if I could lay hands upon it and somehow "read" it. So much for easy dreams of shifting into an Elator and flicking outside the walls, or shifting into an Armiger to carry Silkhands to safety through the air from her window. I could not become a Dragon because I had no pattern for it, nor a Prince, nor a Tragamor. Not unless I could lay hands upon a real one. Which it would be death for Peter to do and highly dangerous for Swallow to attempt. Grimpt? I could, perhaps, go back to that. There were undoubtedly other clothes in the filthy hidey-hole the man had lived in.

But there were other creatures larger than a cat on whom Swallow might lay hands. Horses. The great hunting fustigars from the kennels. There were possibilities there. Well enough. I went back to the loft and spoke to Chance, telling him that I needed to sleep. I said it in a firm voice without begging for help. My pride would not let me do that. If Yarrel would not help me, I would help myself.

Still, the last thought I had was a memory of Yarrel saying that I might get a Talent which would make him hate me. I knew I had already done so, and there was no comfort from that thought. I let Peter sink away from it into swallowing darkness, let Swallow come up again into the quiet of sleep. A few hours until day. It would come soon enough.

11

The Caves of Bannerwell

We awoke to the smell of smoke and food, the clamor of guards and grooms, the pawnish people of the fortress about the business of breakfast, the cackle of fowls, the growling of hungry fustigars. When we had received our slabs of bread and mugs of tea, we sat on the sunwarmed stones while I told Chance and Yarrel what I could do. More important, what I could not. I saw Chance's look of disappointment, but Yarrel's face was as stony as it had been the night before, almost as though he were forbidding himself to have any part in my difficulties. Well, if he would not, he would not. I did not beg him for pity or assistance. If he would be my friend again, he would when he would. I could only wait upon him, and this I owed him for the many times he had waited upon me. So and so and so. It wasn't comforting, but it was all I could do.

"Well then," said Chance. "We'll busy ourselves around the stables. Likely no one will bother us if we are seen grooming horses and mucking out. That will give you time to think more . . ."

"We haven't time," I said. "And I have already thought as much as I can. They gave me to the Divulger because they saw an Elator flick into my dungeon, give me a looking over, then disappear. Would that have been Himaggery's man?"

Chance said, "Himaggery knew where you were.

He had a Pursuivant close enough to Read you. He wouldn't have risked your life so—no. It would have to be someone else."

"Then who? Mandor knew where I was. It was none of his doing, obviously. Mertyn?"

"Unlikely," said Yarrel in a distant voice. "Himaggery had already sent word to Mertyn. He would not have risked your life either, as you well know."

"Then again, who?"

"The High King," said Chance. I stared at him in astonishment. I had never thought of the High King.

"But why? What am I to the High King?"

"You are a person who was with Windlow, that's who. You are a person who was with Silkhands. The Elator may have been looking for her, for Windlow, not for you at all. But the High King would look, wouldn't he? He's a suspecter, that one."

"Having found, what would he do?"

Chance mused. "Get himself into the midst of us one way or another, I'd say. He was set on keeping old Windlow captive, most set. Like a fustigar pup with his teeth in a lure, not going to let go even though there's nothing in it but fur. Likely he's wanting Windlow back again and come here looking for him."

"Windlow will be here," said Yarrel. "When Himaggery comes, Windlow will be with him."

I was dizzy with the thought of it. "So, Himaggery comes from the east, with Mertyn, in such might as they can muster. And the High King comes from the south, also in might. Are there no contingents moving upon us from other directions as well . . ."

Yarrel said coldly, "From what direction might Mavin come, knowing her son is held captive by Mandor?"

I refused to rise to this bait. Being Mavin's son was no fault of mine. I would not be twitted about it. Remembering the dream of the pawns with hayforks, I tried to sympathize with his feelings. "The end of it all will be only blood and fury," I said, as softly and kindly as I could. "First the Gamesmen will kill one another, and then perhaps the pawns will come to kill those of us who are left, if any are left, and there will be more Mandors and more Dazzles to turn death's faces upon the world." I saw their incomprehension. They had not seen Dazzle and Mandor as I had. I tried again. "The Great Game will be a monstrous Death. In which we may all perish. This is not the way to do things. There must be something better."

"Justice," said Yarrel. "Himaggery says we might try that."

"I do not know the word." Indeed, I had never heard it.

"Few do," he answered. "It means simply that the rules do not matter, the Game does not matter so much as that thing which stands above both rules and Game." He went on, becoming passionate as he described what Himaggery had said and what he, himself, had been thinking and dreaming in all his journey from the Bright Demesne—perhaps in his journey since birth. I understood one tenth of it. That tenth, however, was enough to give me an important thought. How important, even I did not know.

"Yarrel, if you believe in this, then why do we not try to do it—try to stop the Game."

"Surely," he sneered. "Ask Mandor to let you and Silkhands go. Ask him to let you both go to Himaggery without Mandor's plotting against Himaggery. Ask the High King to leave Windlow alone. Ask Dazzle to stop building conspiracies against Silkhands. Ask the world to change. Ask that my people be given Justice. All that." His voice was bitter.

"There are those who could not need to ask," I pleaded. "The Immutables, Yarrel. They wouldn't need to ask. If *they* came, then there could be no Game."

There was a long silence. "Why would they come?" he asked at last.

"Perhaps because of this 'Justice' you speak of. Perhaps because their leader's daughter was killed by Mandor and Huld and the pawner. The killers are here. Perhaps because we beg it of them. I don't know why they would come, but I know they will not unless someone asks them, begs them . . ."

"And how may we beg them, we who are prisoners here?"

That piece I had already worked out. "I have an idea," I said, and told them about it. Chance objected to certain things about it, and Yarrel offered a suggestion or two. By the time we were done with our bread and tea, which we had made last longer than any of those around us, we had a plan and my heart was a little lighter. Yarrel had looked at me once without enmity, almost as he used to do. They went off to the stables and I went to offer myself to my taskmaster, the gardener, who was furious that I had not been with him since before dawn. Swallow gaped a witless grin at him and let the words of fury slide away. Within moments he was at the barrow handles once more, on his way to the dung heap.

When he went to get the second barrow-load of the day, Chance signaled from the stable door and Peter rose. I let the barrow rest near the privy, as though I might be inside, and slipped away to the kennels. One of the fustigars lay against the fence, drowsing in the sun, and I laid hands upon her body for long moments before she roused to challenge me. It was enough. I skulked away behind the kennels and went over the fence in the shape of a fustigar, opened the kennel gates in that guise (easy enough even with paws, when the mind inside the beast knew how to do it) and then went among the great, drowsy beasts like a hunter among bunwits. I was mad. My mouth frothed, my growls were deafening as I snapped at flanks, howled, bit, drove them into panic and from panic into wild flight out the open gate. From the stables came the high, screaming whinny of horses similarly driven into fear and flight, and I knew that Chance and Yarrel were at their work getting the horses to the same frenzied pitch as the hunting animals. The fustigars burst across the courtyard in a howling mob, me among them still snapping at hind legs; the horses came out of the stables in a maddened herd, both groups headed straight for the bridge. The lounging Tragamors who guarded it dived out of the way as the animals plunged past them pursued by Yarrel and Chance, pitchforks in their hands, shouting, "Get the horses, don't let the horses get away, grab those horses . . ."

By the time some surly guardsmen were sent in pursuit, Chance and Yarrel were hidden within the forest whistling up their own saddled and laden beasts who had gone unnoticed among the stampeding animals. No one had realized that the two pawns pursuing the horses were not grooms from Mandor's own people. It was true what Yarrel had said. No one paid much attention to pawns.

One fustigar had not gone out with the others. That one slipped behind the kennels from which Swallow emerged, grinning and scratching, so amused by the spectacle that he stayed overlong in the courtyard and had to be summoned back to the gardener.

Armigers went aloft to seek the animals. A Tracker strolled out of the barracks to join others on the bridge. By early afternoon the horses and fustigars were back where they belonged except for two. No one missed the two, or the two pawns who had gone after them. During all this, Peter stayed well down just in case anyone should take it into his head to discover the source of the animals' panic. Distracted as they were by the threat of challenge and Great Game, no one did. There was no hurry, now. The Gathered Waters lay two days' journey east along a good road from Bannerwell. There were little ships crossing it almost daily. Or, one could travel around it to the place of the Immutables on the far side. It would be days before Chance and Yarrel would get there, days more before they could return—or not.

That afternoon Swallow stole some clothing from a washline, the clothing of a steward. He tucked it away where it could be found later and promptly forgot about it. That afternoon the fortress gossiped about an Elator who had appeared in the audience hall and after that in the dungeons. There was much talk of this, and a great deal of movement among the Borderers and other guardsmen. Throughout it all, Swallow fetched manure. When he had eaten his evening meal, he slept, much in need of sleep, and then repeated the previous day's activities. That evening he went to the roof, but saw nothing of importance going on. The third day the same, and on that evening Swallow ceased to be.

On that evening Swallow heard Mandor say to Silkhands that she would be sent to the Divulgers upon the morrow. "To learn who it is who sends these spies among us." Dazzle, leaning against a pillar, heard this threat with enormous and obvious satisfaction. Huld attempted to argue, half-heartedly, as though he knew it would do no good. Silkhands was pale and shaking. As a Healer she knew that they need only leave her in a chill room without sufficient food and she would be unable to Heal herself.

"Why do you do this?" she whispered. "Your thalan knows I make no plot against you! The High King's Demons knew it as well. Yet there is this idiocy among you! What is this madness?"

"If it is madness," Mandor lisped, "then it is what I choose. I *choose* that you be sent to the Divulgers, *Healer.*" His voice was full of contempt and anger, and it was then I knew why he hated Silkhands and why he had hated me. He did not believe that she had secrets or conspiracies against him anymore than he had believed it of me. He simply hated her because she was a Healer who could not Heal him, hated me because I had once loved him and could not love him now. The talk of conspiracies was only talk, only surface, only something to say so that Huld would have an excuse to forgive him without despising him utterly.

The reasons no longer mattered, however. Peter had come up to the surface. Swallow had ceased to be. The half-made plan I had made for the rescue of Silkhands would have to go forward at once, ready or not.

I had observed the stewards as they went about the place bearing food or linens or running errands for Gamesmen of rank. Each wore a coat of dull gray piped in violet and black, Mandor's colors. Swallow had stolen such a coat together with a pair of trousers and soft shoes. I changed into these garments in the orchard as I changed myself to match them, becoming an anonymous steward with an ordinary face. Then I had to watch until the kitchen was almost empty before going into it to pick up a tray with bottle and wine-cup. Only one of the pawnish wenches saw me, and I prayed the face I wore was ordinary enough that one would not notice me particularly. I walked away, staying to the side of the corridors, standing against the wall with my head decently down when Gamesmen went past, bearing the tray as evidence that I belonged where I was, doing what I was doing. When I came to the door of Silkhands' room, it was barred and guarded by a yawning Halberdier. He looked me over casually, without really seeing me, and turned to unbar the door. He did not get up after I hit him with the bottle. It didn't even break. I dragged him behind an arras to take his clothes. He would have a vast headache when awoken, but I was as glad not to have killed him as I was not sorry to have killed Grimpt. He was a simple man with a very small Talent for firemaking and a tiny bit of follow-me. This made him popular among his fellows, but was no reason to wish him ill.

When I went in to Silkhands and told her to come with me, she was hideously frightened. I wanted to tell her not to be afraid, but it was necessary that she feel fear if anyone saw us and felt curious about her. Only if she were truly afraid would the thing work at all, so I put Peter well down into the depths of the Halberdier and let that man escort her into the corridor. We went down a back flight of stairs, along corridors and down yet another flight which brought us into a short hallway off the dining hall. There was still much coming and going though it was very late. Catching Silkhands by the shoulder, I told her roughly to stand quiet. She did so, whimpering. I cursed inside as a group of Gamesmen went past, laughing and quarreling after some late play at cards. Three of them stopped to talk, and I thought they would never go. Then, when they went through the door and away, as I was mentally rehearsing the way to a side door and down through the gardens to the wall, there was an alarm from above. I knew at once they had found the Halberdier.

There was no time left to attempt the escape through the gardens and orchard to the rope over the wall. They would be guarding the walls at the first sound of the alarm. I pulled Silkhands to me and hissed, "If you wish to live, be silent. If you truly wish to live, think of being grass as once you did upon a canyon side with Chance beside you . . ."

She searched my face, then said, "Peter." I do not know how she could have known so quickly who it was, except that my hands were on her and she could see into the body I wore. Perhaps it had some distinctive feel to it that she recognized. She was quick and compliant, however, for she stopped gaping at once and let her face go blank. I knew she was doing everything she could to be invisible if Huld sought her.

The surface mind of the Halberdier knew the castle well, but I could find no sure hiding place in those memories. Then I remembered the words of Huld and Mandor when they spoke of Grimpt. The Caves of Bannerwell. Where? The Halberdier did not know, but Grimpt knew. I sought the pattern of that memory once more, pulled it back into being. Oh, yes, Grimpt had known well. There was the way, the rusty door, the key, the cobweb hung tunnels . . .

I did not wait to explore the memory or understand it. Instead, I turned back the way we had come and tugged Silkhands into a stumbling run. Here was a panel which opened to a secret pressure. Here was a door hidden behind a tapestry. Here were cobwebby stairs hidden within walls which led downward to that same torture dungeon toward which Grimpt had led Peter those long days before.

We did not stay to examine the instruments there. The place was empty though a torch burned smokily on the wall. The way in Grimpt's memory lay through a half-hidden door, its metal surface splotched with corruption, the hinges red with rust, the key in the lock. It opened protestingly, the hinges screaming, and we stepped within to lock the door behind us. I had known the way would be dark so had taken up the torch to light our way down into the belly of the earth. There was no sound. Our footsteps were pillowed in dust and our panting breaths lost themselves in the vaulted height above. Silkhands followed, her face still carefully blank until I shook her and said, "There is stone between us and the world, Silkhands. We cannot be Read here." Then she sighed and almost fainted upon my arm, and I knew it was from holding her breath for endless moments.

"How did you find this place?" she whispered. "Where does it go?"

"I don't know," I confessed.

"You're a Shifter," she said, almost accusingly. I was reminded of Yarrel's tone. "You did turn out to be a Shifter, like your mother."

"You knew about my mother?"

"Himaggery found out. Before we came after you. He said it would make no difference if I knew, for Mandor already knew of it. How did you find this place?"

"I took the shape of one who knew. The memory came with the form."

"Ah," she said. "It's like Healing, then."

"Is it? I suppose it must be. Like Healing. Like Reading. It feels to me as though several of those things are going on, all at once."

"Where do we go now?"

I laughed, then wanted to cry. "Silkhands, I don't know. I don't know what this place is, or why Huld thought of it as a hiding place or why Grimpt knew of it. I only knew we needed to get away, and this was available. It seemed better than being given to the Divulgers."

"Well," she offered, "if you don't know, then we must find out."

So we explored. We did not fear losing our way for we could always follow our own footprints in the dust to go back the way we had come. That dust, undisturbed for ages, indicated that we were in no frequently traveled place. It was almost a maze, winding corridors with niches and side aisles and rooms. After a very long time, during which we went down and then up and then down again, we came to an opening into a great open space filled with tombs, a veritable city of tombs. They stretched away from the torchlight in an endless series to a high, far line of lights, dim, fiery, as though of windows into a firelighted place.

"Could we have come under the walls?" Silkhands

asked me. "If this is the place Bannerwell gives its dead, then there must be another entrance, one better suited to processions."

She was right. Funeral pomp and display would require a ceremonial entrance of some kind, something with ornamental gates and wide corridors. "If we could find it," I whispered, "it would probably be well guarded. And I don't feel that we are outside the walls . . ."

"How had you planned to get us out?" She laughed when I told her. "Down a rope? Well, it might have worked. I was fearful enough to risk my life down a rope. Why did you not shift into an Armiger and carry us away?"

I told her that I did not because I could not, and she became very curious, full of questions, while we both stood in the land of tombs and the torch burned low. I wanted to hug her and slap her at once. There was no time for this, for this chatter, no time and I couldn't decide what was best to do. As was often the case, while I dithered and Silkhands talked, events moved upon us. There was a booming noise from the far, high firelit spaces, an enormous gonging sound, then a creaking of hinges. One of the firelit spaces began to enlarge, torches starring the space behind it.

"There is your ceremonial gate," I said. "They've come to search for us."

"And we've left prints in the dust a blind man could follow!"

"No," I said. "We'll leave nothing behind us. Turn and see." Grimpt's small Talent for moving was enough. The dust rose in little fountains and settled once more, even as a carpet. We turned and ran, little dust puffs following us like the footfalls of a ghost. I thought of Ghost Pieces and of the surrounding dead and shuddered, glad I had seen no Necromancer in Bannerwell. "Try to remember which turns we make," I

panted. "When they have gone, if they go, we'll try to
find our way back." She saved her breath for running,
but I knew she heard me. We twisted, backtracked
down a parallel way, then down a branching hall, into a
small tomb chamber, then into an alcove behind a
carved cenotaph. "The torch must go out," I said. "Else
they'll find us by the light."

"Gamelords," she sighed. "I hate the dark."

"It's all right. I can light it again." I blessed the Halberdier and was glad once more that I had not killed
him. He knew enough to light the torch, thus I could do
it when I had to. We crouched in the blanketing dark.
They would not be able to Read us through the stone, or
track us by eye, but they might use fustigars. Indeed, we
heard baying rise and fade, rise and fade again. "They
cannot smell our way in this dust," I said. "Our tracks
are gone. They cannot find us . . ."

I had spoken too soon. The sound of the animals grew
nearer, and we waited, poised to run. As I rose to my
feet, I caught the string of my pouch on a stone and it
snapped. Some half-dozen of the tiny Gamesmen fell to
the floor. I felt for them with my hands, cursing the
darkness, gathering them up one by one. I had heard
one of them fall to my left, groped for it, found it at last
and gripped it tightly just as a beam of light went by the
entrance to the tomb chamber out of which our alcove
opened. It grew warm in my grasp, warmer, hot. Almost
I dropped it, then opened my hand to find it shining in
the dark, the tiny Necromancer glowing like a small star
on my palm.

I closed my hand to hide the light. It spoke to me. It
said, "I am Dorn, Raiser of the Dead, Master of all my
kind . . ." A pattern was there, complex as a tapestry,
knotted and interwoven, vast and ramified as root and
branch of a mighty tree. It did not wait for me to Read it
or take it. It flowed into me and would have done even if
I had tried to stop it or dam it away. Silkhands gasped,

for the Gamespiece shone between my fingers so that
the flesh seemed transparent. Far away was the yammer
of voices and animals. I only half heard it as I dropped
the piece back into the pouch. It was no longer glowing.

The searchers were returning. They paused at the entrance to the tomb room and began to come inside. I
heard Huld calling to them from a distance. "Search every room. Mark every corridor to show you have
searched . . ." They could not fail to see us if they came
inside as those obedient forms began to do, long shadows reaching ahead of them in the torchlight. Something within me sighed, deeply.

Between us and the searchers were seven tombs,
cubes of marble set with golden crowns. Here lay some
past rulers of Bannerwell, some Princes or Kings of time
long gone. I sighed once more, the Dorn pattern within
me beginning to Read time, back and back again, taking
measure from the stone in which the dead Kings lay,
back into their lives, taking up their dust, their bones,
the rotted threads in which they were clad, making all
whole again as though living, to rise up, up from the sep-
ulchre into the air, a shade, a spirit, a ghastly King
peering down upon these intruders out of shadowy eyes,
speaking with a voice in which the centuries cried like
lost children in a barren place, "Who comes, who
comes, who comes . . ."

Beside me Silkhands hid her face and screamed silently into her hands. Before me the searchers drew up,
eyes wide, each mouth stretched into a rictus of fear.
The fustigars cowered, and the spirit confronted them,
"Who comes, who comes, who comes," as yet another
rose beside him, and then one more, and yet again and
again.

The searchers fled and the spirit heads began to turn
toward the place we hid. Within me came the sigh, and
Dorn let them rest once more. Now I knew why Dazzle
had so feared the threat of her dead. These had been no

dead of mine, and yet I feared, for out of these had come a hungering and a thirst which my life would not have slaked. One who raised these dead raised terror. And yet, even as I knew this, I knew that Dorn could hold them so they did no harm, or loose them, as Dorn would.

I comforted Silkhands, blindly, babbling. "Himaggery told me to keep the Gamespieces safe. To keep them to myself. Well did he say so. I wish I had buried them back once more in the earth."

"We are alive," she whispered, practical and fearful at once. "I would rather be alive, even sweating like this. Having seen death, I would rather be alive."

"I can raise them up again, if we need to . . ."

"Not now," she begged. "I am so tired. I have been afraid for so long. Not now."

We lit the torch and followed the footprints of those who had fled, but the hope of escape was vain. The great room of tombs was lit with a thousand torches and there were watchers at every corner of it. I could Read Mandor in the room, glowing with anger. I could read Dazzle there, as well, writhing thoughts, like a nest of serpents twining upon one another in incestuous frenzy. A telltale tickle at the edge of my mind pushed me back behind a towering midfeather which held up the groined ceiling. I hugged Silkhands to me. "We can't stay here. Huld is searching for us. We need stone between us and him . . ."

My words were interrupted by a fury of sound, drums throbbing, a wild clatter of wheels, and a thunder upon the bridge. Trumpets called. Silkhands said, "So, someone has come to give Mandor a Great Game. Those are the last of the wood wagons being driven across the bridge with fuel for the ovens . . ."

We heard Mandor scream instructions at the guards. The doors clanged shut and there was a scurry of purposeful movement. We withdrew into the shadows of the corridor. "I have not slept in days," said Silkhands. "If we may not get out, let us hide away and rest. I cannot Heal myself of this weariness much longer, and I am hungry . . ."

I was hungry, too, and we had nothing with us to eat or drink. As for sleep, however, that we could do. We went from squared and vaulted rooms into dim bat-hung halls where dawn light filtered down from grilled shafts twenty manheights above us, and from there into darker corridors lined with vaults bearing each the sign and legend of him who slept there. At last we found a high, dry shelf three-quarters hidden behind hanging stone pillars down which water dripped endlessly in a mournful cadence. There we would be hidden by stone in all directions, hidden by shadow, hidden by sleep. We shared the last of Windlow's herb and fixed our minds upon peace. Lost in the darkness of the place of tombs, we slept.

12

Mavin

I woke to a clicking sound, a small, almost intimate sound in the vastness of that stone pillared cave. It reminded me of the death beetle we had often heard in the long nights in School House, busy in the rafters, the click, click, click timing the life of the Tower as might the ticking of a clock. I was still half asleep when I peered over the edge of the ledge we lay upon. The cavern drifted in pale light, mist strewn, and at the center of it a woman was sitting in a tall, wooden chair, knitting.

She had not been there before. I had not heard her arrive. For the moment I thought it was a dream and pinched myself hard enough to bring an involuntary exclamation, half throttled. Silkhands heard it, wakened to it, sat up suddenly, saying, "What is it? Oh, what is it?" Then she, too, heard the sound and peered at the distant figure, her expression of blank astonishment mirroring my own.

Before I could answer her, if I had had any answer to give, the woman looked up toward us and called, "You may as well come down. It will make conversation easier." Then she returned to her work, the needles in her hands flashing with a hard, metallic light. I stared away in the direction we had entered this vault. Nothing. All was silence, peace, no trumpets, no drums, no torches. Finally, I heaved myself down from the ledge and helped Silkhands as we climbed down to the uneven floor of the cave. The clicking was now interspersed with a creaking sound, the sound of the chair in which the woman sat, rocking to and fro. Once, long, long ago I had seen some such chair. I could not remember when. The yarn she used frothed between her hands as though alive, pouring from the needles in a flood which spread its loose loops over her knees and cascaded to the stone. The speed of her knitting increased to a whirling rattle, the creaking of the chair faster and faster, like a bellows breathing, until she was finished all at once. She flung the completed work onto the stone before her where it lay like a pile of woolen snow.

"What have you made?" asked Silkhands, doubtfully. I knew she was unable to think of anything else to say. I could think of nothing at all. The woman fixed us with great, inhuman eyes, yellow and bright as those of a bird.

"I have knitted a Morfus," she said in a deep voice. "Soon it will get up and go about its work, but just now it is resting from the pain of being created." The piled fabric before her shivered as she spoke, and I thought it moaned. "Would you care for some cabbage?" the woman asked.

Silkhands said, "I would be very grateful for anything to eat, madam. I am very hungry." When she spoke, my mouth filled with saliva, even though I hated cabbage raw or cooked and always had. The woman found a cabbage somewhere beside herself in the chair and offered it. Silkhands tore off a handful of leaves.

The woman said, "It is better than nothing. Although I do not like it as it is." She stared intently at the vegetable in her hand, turning it this way and that. It fuzzed before my eyes, fuzzed, misted, became a roasted fowl. The pile of fabric moaned once more, sat up, extended long, knitted tentacles and pushed itself erect. Vaguely manshaped, it swayed where it stood, featureless and without much substance. I could see through it in spots.

An impatient snort from the woman brought my attention back to her. She had given the fowl to Silkhands. "Try this instead. Tell me if it tastes right."

Silkhands tore a leg from the fowl and took a bit of it, wiping her face on her arm, nodding. "It tastes . . . only a little like cabbage."

"Ah. Well, then, it's an improvement. Still, you could do much better, being a Healer, if that lazy youth would help you."

"I don't understand," said Silkhands, remembering at last to offer me some of the fowl. "What do you mean, I could do better?"

"Have you ever Healed a chicken?" the woman asked.

"Never."

"Ah. Well then, perhaps you could not do as well as I have done. If you had ever Healed a chicken, you would know how the flesh is made. And if that boy were to Read you as you thought about that, then he could change the cabbage far better than I have done."

"Pardon, madam," I said. "But I have not that Talent."

"Nonsense. You have all the Talents there are, from Dorn to Didir, or from Didir to Dorn, as the case may be. You have the Gamesmen of Barish, I know it. Even if I had not felt the spirit of Dorn moving in the corridors of the earth like a waking thunder I would still have known. Was it not Seen? Was it not foretold? Why else am I here and are you where you are?"

"The Gamesmen of Barish?" By this time I was certain that I still slept, dreaming in the high stone wall on the little ledge. "I don't know what you . . ."

"These," she flicked a knitting needle at me, catching the loop of my pouch and rattling the Gamesmen within it. "These. You have already taken Dorn into being. Soon you must take others, or if not soon then late. By the seven hells, you're not afraid of them are you, boy?"

"Afraid? Of *them?* Them . . . who?"

"Witless," she commented acidly, looking me over from head to foot as though she could not believe what she saw. "Witless and spitless, no more juice than a parsnip. By the seven hells, boy, you raised up the ancient Kings of Bannerwell. How did you think you did that? Did you perhaps whittle them up out of a bit of wood and your little knife? Or whistle them up like a wind? Or brew them, perhaps, like tea? How did you do it, gormless son of an unnamed creation? Hmmm? Answer me!"

I was beginning to be very angry. As I grew wider awake and even slightly less hungry (the fowl was filling, though it did taste like cabbage), I became angrier by the moment. I was distracted, however, for at that moment the Morfus decided to do whatever it was a Morfus did. Moaning shrilly, it staggered off toward one side of the great cavern and began to climb the stone. It lurched and flapped like laundry upon a slack line, wavering and lashing itself upward.

"At this rate, it'll never get there," she commented as she took up the needles and the wool once more to pour out another long confusion of knitting upon her lap. "You haven't answered me," she said. 'How did you think you raised them up, boy? By what means?"

"I raised them up by using the pattern I found in one of the Gamespieces," I said, stiffly. "By accident."

"No more by accident than trees grow by accident. Trees grow because it is their nature to do so. The Gamespieces of Barish were designed to have a nature of their own—to lie long hidden until a time when they would fall into the hands of one who could use them." There was a long pause and then she said in a slightly altered tone, "No. That is not quite correct. They would fall into the hands of one who would use them *well*. That is tricky. Perhaps a bit of fear and confusion would not be amiss under those circumstances." The knitting

poured from her lap onto the floor and lay there, quivering. Then the knitted creature heaved itself upward to
stagger toward its companion which still struggled upward against the far rock wall.

Silkhands had been observing the woman narrowly,
and now she seated herself at the knitter's feet and laid
hand upon her knee. The woman started, then com-
posed herself and smiled. "Ah, so you'd find out what
goes on, would you, Healer? Well, stay out of my head
and the rest of me be thy play-pen. There's probably
some work or other needs doing in there."

"What are the Gamesmen of Barish?" I asked.
"Please stop confusing me. I think you're doing it pur-
posely, and it doesn't help me. Just tell me. What are
the Gamesmen of Barish?"

She rose, incredibly tall and thin, like a lath, I
thought, then changed that thought. Like a sword, lean
and keen-edged and pointed. She laughed as though she
Read that thought. "Long ago," she chanted, "in a time
forgotten by all save those who read books, were two
Wizards named Barish and Vulpas. You've heard of
them? Ah, of course. You've heard of them from the
self-styled Historian." She laughed, almost kindly.
"These two had a Talent which was rare. They called it
Wisdom. Or, so it is said by some. They caused the Immutables, you know. They learned the true nature of
the Talents. They codified many things which had been
governed until then, in approximately equal parts, by
convention and superstition. Those who lived by convention and superstition could not bear that matters of
this kind be brought into the light, and so they sought
out Barish and Vulpas with every intention of killing
them.

"Later the Guardians announced that Barish and
Vulpas were dead. There was much quiet rejoicing.
However, there are books which one may read today (if
one knows where to find them) which were written by

Barish and Vulpas many years after the Guardians announced their deaths. Could it be the Guardians lied? Who is to say. It was long ago, after all . . ."

"The Gamesmen," I said firmly.

"Barish claimed," she went on, "that the pattern of a Talent—nay, of a whole personality, could be encoded into a physical object and then Read from that object as it could be Read in a man, by one with the ability to do so."

"That would be utter magic," said Silkhands.

"Some may say so," the knitter said. "While others would say otherwise. Nonetheless, the *books* say that Barish made his claim manifest in the creation of a set of Gamesmen. There are eleven *different* pieces in the set, embodying, so it is written, the Talents of the forebears."

"Why?" I breathed, ideas surging into my head all at once. "Why would he have done this thing? It's true, Silkhands. I know it's true. It was exactly like Reading a person. I felt Dorn, felt him sigh. It was he who raised the spectres up, not me. How terrible and wonderful. But why would he do it?" I babbled this nonsense while the knitter fixed me with her yellow eyes and the Morfuses clambered ever higher against the stones.

"If Barish was able to code the Talents in this way, then he must also have been able to perceive them for himself. In which case, he would have perceived the Talent of Sorah, Seer. Perhaps through Sorah he saw something in the future. Who can say? It was very long ago."

"You are saying that the Wizard did this thing long ago so that someone—Peter—could use these Talents now?" Silkhands seemed to be asking a question, but it was directed more at me than at the knitter, sounded more like a demand than a query. "So that Peter can use them," she repeated. What did she want me to do? Gamelords! She seemed to want something, Yarrel wanted something else, Mertyn another thing, Mandor something else again. While I . . . what in the name of the seven devils did I want? Nothing. I wanted to do nothing. Nothing at all. Doing things was frightening. Every time I had done anything at all decisive, I had been terrified.

I said it to Silkhands, praying she would understand. "When I heard Dorn sigh within me, I was afraid . . ."

The knitter interrupted. "But you knew Dorn could control the Ghosts. You knew you could do it."

"I knew someone could. Someone. But it didn't feel like me."

"Aha," she chortled, rocking so hard that the wood of the chair began to creak in ominous protest. "You felt you were someone else, did you? And when Grimpt cracked Grimpt's skull and put him down the oubliette? Hmmm? Who did that?"

"No one knows about that," I said, horrified. "No one at all."

"No one except those who *do* know about it. Watchers. Morfuses. Seers. Bitty things with eyes that peer from crannies and cracks."

Silkhands said, "Who is Grimpt?"

"Ahh, shh, shh, we've upset him enough. Poor boy. All this Talent throbbing away at his fingertips and he doesn't know where to put his hands."

What was I to say. She was right. I had the Talent in my mind or in the pouch at my belt to fling Mandor and all his house into the nethermost north, into the deepest gorge of the Hidamans. All I needed was a source of power great enough . . . and even with ordinary power, the heat in the stone beneath me, I could summon up legions of the dead and was afraid to do so. "You've a poor tool in me," I said. "A poor tool indeed. Dorn terrified me. Sorah would probably petrify me. Why couldn't I have been a pawn, like Yarrel. I'd have been a good pawn, moved about by others . . ."

"Better a poor tool than an evil one," she said. Then she reached out to touch me for the first time, and it was as though I had been lightning struck. "You've been too long in the nursery, boy. Too long with lads and dreamers and cooks. Come out, come out wherever you are! The cock crows morning, and the Great Game is toward! Play it or be swept from the board."

From high above came a keening howl, a ghost noise, like wind down a chimney. We looked up to see the Morfuses' black shapes against a glow of sky. They had found a way out and called to us of their discovery.

"There it is," said the knitter. "The way out. You can go that way if you like. Sit on a pile of stone up there on Malplace Mountain and watch the Game. Or, you can go out through the funeral doors to the tombs, out with a host behind you." She was across the floor and up the wall like a spider, arms, legs, head all a blur as she moved toward those two figures high on the wall. "It's your choice, boy. Mothers should not force their young. It's bad for personal development . . ."

"Who," I rasped, choking. "Who . . . who are you . . ."

"Mavin Manyshaped, boy. Here to cheer you with two of your cousins."

The Morfus shapes before the light flickered and changed before us. Now there were only two slim youths grinning down at us out of glittering eyes, flame-red hair falling across their faces. Then they were out of the hole and gone, her behind them, so quickly gone there was no time to say anything. Mavin—Mother. And two Shapeshifter cousins, children, that meant, of Mavin's sister or sisters. And a way out. High and pure through that sunny hole came the sound of a trumpet calling "To Air, To Air" for the Armigers. A drum answered from a hillside, "Thawum, Thawum," signal to the Tragamors, "move, move."

"Oh, hells," I giggled hysterically. "Who is doing battle with whom? Is it Himaggery? Or the High King? Or merely some trickery of a Shapechanger who says she bore me . . ."

Silkhands cried, "Oh, Peter, if you're going to go all sensitive and nervous, this isn't a good time for it at all."

I screamed at her, screamed at her like a market stall woman or a mule driver, thrust her before me up the rocky slope until she was pushed half out of the opening, half laughing, half crying at me. "Be damned, Healer," I shouted at her. "It isn't you has to do the things you expect me to do. Go out there and watch the Game, you silly thing, you chatter-bird. Go, go out, out of here and leave me alone . . ."

Then I tumbled back down the rock wall into the bottom of the cavern to lie face down on the stones, weeping miserably and feeling that never, never in my fifteen years of life had I been understood by anyone at all.

After which I went and raised up the dead.

13

The Great Game

I must leave myself again to tell you what I later learned
had happened to others. I must go back to Himaggery's
realm, back to the fourteenth day of my captivity. An
Elator arrived from Schooltown to tell of Mertyn's arrival only hours before he himself arrived.

I have visualized that arrival many times. King
Mertyn, in a dusty cloak, his travel hat stained with rain,
beard floured with the dirt of the road, riding into the
courtyard of the High Demesne among the mists and the
blossoms. They offered him time to bathe before he
came to Himaggery, and he refused it. He came into the
audience hall to find Himaggery awaiting him, not
seated upon his chair, elevated, but standing alone without servitors by the door. The two had not met before.

And the King used his Talent. He used Beguilement
upon Himaggery, a fatal charm, a deadly charisma.
Standing in that room of power, where no chill might
rob him of the full use of that Talent which was his, he
used it as he had not used it in his life theretofore. So he
has told me, his thalan, since that time. He wagered his
life upon being able to charm Himaggery into doing
what the King wished.

And Himaggery laughed. He laughed, clasped
Mertyn by the hand, and led him to a table where he offered him a wash basin full of hot water, a towel, and
foods steaming from the kitchens.

"You need not beguile me, King. I will help you without all that charm. I will help you because I believe it is right to do so, though I am less sure of that than of some few other things. Our cause, however, seems to be the cause of Justice."

Mertyn was better educated than many of his fellows. He had, after all, been a student of Windlow, as had Himaggery. Unlike Prionde, the High King, he had listened to Windlow, had even understood some of what he was taught. Thus, when he heard Himaggery use the word "justice" he recognized the word, and with that recognition came a sense of peace.

"My friend," he said solemnly, "forgive me. I thought to protect my thalan, Peter, through his early years. Who knows? Perhaps I hoped to protect him throughout his life, though we know that in the Game such things are impossible. I have broken many rules. I am paying for that now, perhaps, in being consumed with fear for the boy. I never called him by any name of kinship. I tried to warn him away from that kindermar, Mandor. At the end, I only tried to save him, and I might as well have thrust him into Mandor's hands. Have you any news of him?" Despite all dignity, I am told, his eyes were wet.

"Shh, shh, I understand," said Himaggery. "I had no sisters, thus have had no thalan, but there are young ones I have loved and cared for and fretted over in the dark hours. Yes. I have word brought by an Elator from Bannerwell who has it from a Pursuivant I have stationed there. The boy is imprisoned. He has been harshly treated, but he is not seriously hurt. Which is not to say he may not be hurt at some future time, though the Seers of this Demesne think not. Windlow thinks not, Mertyn."

"Windlow? Here? Oh, how did he come here? How did he manage to escape from Prionde? How wonderful. I wish to see him, Wizard, soon. What a wonderful thing . . ."

And see him he did. Do not think that they were all careless of me, but they were not willing to take impetuous action which might endanger me further. They knew where I was, that I was watched hour on hour, and that I was in great despair, but they knew I wouldn't die of it. Each of them had been equally despairing at one time or another, and each of them had survived it. So, while they plotted and planned to come to Bannerwell for my sake, they plotted and planned for other reasons as well.

"Whether Peter were held by Mandor or not, it would still be necessary to wage Great Game against him, Mertyn." So said Windlow. "We have learned from his mind and from Peter's that the Prince is thinking of linkages . . ."

Mertyn looked thoughtful and curious at once, nodding for the Wizard to say on.

"Mandor believes he can get himself a new body through some use of linkages. So my spies Read. He has in mind a linkage of Demon and Shapechanger. He has not thought it through. He has not studied or read, for which we may be grateful. Instinct guides him, and it guides him too far. If he had thought more, he would have included a Healer in the group as the Talent most likely to manipulate the tissues of a brain to accommodate him. *We are grateful that he has not thought,* King. He has as yet had no success. Even a small success may show him how limited his imagination has been."

"I seem to remember that you mentioned linkages to me long and long ago," Mertyn said to Windlow. "It was something you believed was possible . . ."

"It is something I know is possible," the old man replied. "Himaggery has done it. You should have seen it, Mertyn. It was quite wonderful. Demon linked to

Pursuivant linked to Elator—with a few Rancelmen mixed in for flavor. They found Peter in Bannerwell in two days. If we had not allowed ourselves to be misled by a few false handmarks, we would have found him in one day. Truly remarkable. And it is only one of an infinite number of things we can do . . ."

"Only one of many things which are possible," corrected Himaggery. "We have done only a few. The possibilities are wide, as Windlow says, and terrifying. Half the things I dream up frighten me out of my wits. But I trust me more than I trust this Mandor, though that, too, is terrifying."

"Believe me," said Mertyn, "you are wise to do so. I have known of Prince Mandor since he was a child. If there was a simple way to do a thing which would not hurt or kill, he would eschew it in favor of some complex scheme which would maim and mutilate. If there was an honorable thing to do, he would do the opposite. He so conducted himself in the Games of his youth that he had a dozen sworn enemies of great power by the time he was twenty-seven. They were ready to descend upon Bannerwell, to obliterate it forever, with all its long history and the tombs of its lineage. Then Mandor's thalan, Huld, a Demon of good reputation, a Gamesman of honor, prevailed upon the young Prince to go into the Schooltown as a Gamesmaster for a time. It was thought that this sequestering of the young man in a place where he was honor bound not to use his Talent would allow matters time to cool, insults to be forgotten, enemies to become merely un-friends rather than rabid warriors. So it might have done.

"But Mandor could not occupy the post of Gamesmaster with honor, or even patience, though it was needful to save his life. He behaved toward Peter as he had always behaved, as he will always behave. There is something warped in him . . ." Mertyn sighed.

"There is nothing more warped in him than in many," said Himaggery heatedly. "Any Gamesman who eats up a dozen pawns during an evening's Game has no more honor than Mandor . . ."

Mertyn nodded. "You say it. I might say it. Windlow, you, I know, would say it. Does the world say it? No. Pawns are pawns for the eating. That is what the world says."

"I am in my own world," said Himaggery. "You, Mertyn, may follow the outer world, but I will make my own. And the knowledge of what can be done with link-ages must not come into Mandor's hands. So. It is neces-sary that Great Game be called. He must be distracted from this obsession. If necessary, he must be de-stroyed."

"And how will you mount Game against him? He is in his home place. Undoubtedly his battle ovens are erected, his fuel wagons running to and fro from dawn to dawn. You will be far from your home, far from this source of power. He will have an advantage."

"*I* will have the advantage," whispered Himaggery. "And I will use only a hundredth of it. If I were to use it all, the world could not stand against me."

" 'Ware, Himaggery," said Windlow, sternly. " 'Ware the demands of pride."

"Oh, I am safe enough, old one. For now, at least." He laughed, a little bitterly. "Though you may need to watch me in the future."

Then it was that Himaggery, Windlow, and the King began their work. From all the surrounding area Gamesmen were summoned by Elators to attend upon the Bright Demesne. The Tragamors and Sorcerers who came were many, more than King Mertyn had ever seen in one place.

"Why Tragamors?" he asked. "I can understand Sor-cerers, but most Games of this kind depend more heavily upon Armigers than upon Tragamors . . ."

"We will have Armigers when we need them," Himaggery replied in a grim voice. "But we do not need them here. They go toward Bannerwell even now, in small groups, within the forest. As do other Tragamors than those you see here and other Sorcerers, as well. Every one I have been able to recruit during the last decade."

"I did not know your Demesne counted so many Gamesmen among its followers."

"It were better that none knew, and well that as few were aware as possible. For that reason, we have had no panoply, no Gamely exercises. What we have learned to do, we have learned in private, and only those safe from the needs of pride have learned with us. It would take only one braggart in a Festival town to have given our secret to the world."

"What is it you have learned?"

"You will see soon enough. It is easier to see than to explain. We have not yet had enough practice at any part of it. I have been at some pains to keep triflers and troublemakers far from this Demesne. Some, like Dazzle and Borold, two I tolerated out of affection for Silkhands, were sent away on errands of one kind or another if they insisted upon attaching themselves to me. Others I have sent on long journeys. Still, I have always had the fear we would be betrayed."

"And where is Dazzle now?" asked Windlow.

"Gone. Gone after Silkhands, still seeking to do harm to her who would only have wished her well. I should have stopped her, should have . . . well. I was thinking of other things."

And he went on thinking of other things, though not for long, for on that afternoon, the eighteenth of my captivity, an Elator arrived from Bannerwell to tell them that Silkhands had been taken prisoner after being denounced by Dazzle and Borold. And on the day after that, still another messenger arrived to say that Chance and Yarrel had fled from Bannerwell, but that Silk-hands was still held there.

It was on that day that Himaggery's legions began the march to Bannerwell, though it was like no march Mertyn had seen before. There was a monstrous wagon piled with many huge, curved shields of metal, polished to a mirror gleam. And there were all those Tragamors in the train. And the way was always starting and stop-ping, with a curved shield taken off the wagon each place the march stopped, each with a Sorcerer to attend it and at least two Tragamors, though in places there were three or even four. In each spot was a wait while the shield was "tested" while Mertyn fretted and old Windlow lay in his wagon, soft pillowed in quilts, watching the sky. This testing seemed to take eternities, and Mertyn grumbled and sweated, furious that Himaggery would not tell him what was being done.

"I cannot," said Himaggery. "You might well think about it if I told you, and Mandor may have Demons Reading the road."

"Aren't you thinking about it?"

Himaggery laughed. "Does the stonemason think of cutting stone as he does so? His hands know what to do. He thinks of his dinner or of going fishing. That's what I think of. Going fishing."

It was true that all those in the train seemed well prac-ticed at what they did. Their road lay straight across the Middle River, with the first stop made across the lake from the Bright Demesne. Then, each successive stop was in a straight line from the previous one. Where there were hills, a mirror was placed atop each. The nineteenth day of my captivity passed (for I still counted the captivity as I later numbered it for all the time I was in Bannerwell), and the twentieth, and the twenty-first.

During all this time the legions of Himaggery drew closer to Bannerwell, but slowly, a crawling pace which wearied and fretted all within the train. On each morning and evening came a messenger from Bannerwell to say that the ovens were built, that the wood wagons thundered in across the bridge, that the fortress was furnished against siege, that Armigers, Sorcerers, Elators, and Tragamors were assembled with more still coming in. And still Himaggery did not hurry, did not increase his pace. They went on, the shield wagon growing less and less heavily laden, the vast number of Sorcerers and Tragamors dwindling day by day.

And on the evening of the twenty-second day of my captivity, word arrived at Himaggery's tent that Silkhands was to be given to the Divulgers but that she had thwarted Mandor by disappearing.

"I should think," Windlow told them thoughtfully, "that Peter is involved in this. Though my Talent grows dim with age and faulty with time, I seem to See something of that boy in this whole affair. He is all mixed up somehow with Divulgers and manure piles, but the feel of him is still unmistakably Peter, moving about in Bannerwell or beneath it. I am sure of it."

Himaggery laughed silently until tears came to his eyes. "You would advise us not to worry?"

"Oh, worry by all means," said Windlow. "By all means. Yes. It sharpens the wits. A good worry does wonders for the defensive capabilities of the brain. However, I should not advise you to do without sleep."

Mertyn said, "Somehow, that doesn't help, old teacher. I think it will affect my ability to sleep . . ."

To which Windlow replied, "I think I have an herb here somewhere which will . . ." And so they slept that night, not overlong, but well.

On the morning came yet another messenger to tell

them the most astonishing news. The trumpets and drums of Bannerwell beat summons to air, to move, because upon the surrounding hills had come a mighty host to call Great Game upon Bannerwell, no other than the followers of the High Demesne and the High King himself. It was those same drums and trumpets which I heard as I drove Silkhands out of the caves in a fury. The High King had come to Bannerwell. And why?

Why, he had come to take Windlow back with him, for he believed the old man was held captive in the Bannerwell dungeons.

What followed was something Silkhands saw from her place on Malplace Mountain, watching the Game as Mavin had suggested, crying to herself, and talking, as she watched.

You must see Bannerwell as she saw it. Below Malplace Mountain the river curves down from the north, swoops into a graceful loop before swinging north once more, then turning eastward through Havajor Dike and across the fertile plains to the Gathered Waters. In that loop of river stands a low, curved cliff upon which the walls of the fortress are built to follow the same line, so that cliff and wall are one. On the west the Tower rises from the wall in one unbroken height, on the south the green of the orchard close feathers the walltop with the roofs and spires behind it. From her place on Malplace Mountain, Silkhands could look down into the courtyard to see it packed full of Gamesmen with more upon the walls and the roofs. On the north, hidden by the bulk of the castle, was the shield wall and bridge, and outside that the moat which extended from the Banner on one side to the Banner on the other side, across the whole neck of the looped river. The bridge was up, the gate was down. Any further messages would be carried by Heralds; there was no further need for a bridge.

Then, see upon the hills to the north of Bannerwell a great host of Gamesmen and horses and machines centered upon a cluster of tents with a high, red tent in the midst of them. Here was the High King among his people. Between the moat and the hills was another host under the banner of some tributary Prince to the High King, and still more allies were assembled between these multitudes and the stony dike. This great host had come upon Bannerwell from the north, an unexpected direction, and waited now as Game was called upon Prince Mandor. The trumpets were still shivering when Silkhands came onto the ledge.

It is part of the Talent of a Herald to Move the air about him in such a way that all within the Demesne may hear each word which is spoken. So Silkhands, even at that distance, could hear plainly when the Herald of the High King rode to the edge of the moat and cried:

"All within reach of my voice pay heed, all within reach of my voice give ear, for I speak for the High King, he of the High Demesne, most puissant, most terrible, who comes now in might to call Great Game against Mandor, styled Prince of Bannerwell, who has in most unprincely fashion given sanctuary to traitorous and miscreant pawns, abductors of the old, holders for base ransom the valued friend of Prionde, High King.

"I speak of Windlow the Seer, formerly of Windlow's House, Schoolhouse to the High Demesne.

"So says the High King: That Windlow shall be sent forth with honor and in good array, that those who abducted him shall be put forth, dishonored and bound, and that Mandor, styled Prince, shall pay the cost of all the array here massed against him and his Demesne, else shall Great Game proceed . . ."

"Gamelords," whispered Silkhands. "It's Borold with Mandor." She could see Mandor on the battlement, three figures beside him. Huld, Borold, and Dazzle. Now the trumpets of Mandor sounded and Borold rose higher than the tower to look down upon the High King's host as he cried the response of Bannerwell.

"All within sound of my voice pay heed, all within reach of my voice give ear, for I speak for Prince Mandor of Bannerwell. My Prince is not unwilling to meet Great Game with those who have challenged him or those whom he has taken pains to offend. But he begs of the High King an indulgence, that they may speak together with their attendant Demons in order that the High King be sure of the grounds of his offense e'er Game is called . . ."

Then was a long silence during which the Herald of the High Demesne spoke with the High King, as did others of his train, until at last the drums on the hills beat thrice, "thawum, thawum, thawum," and were answered from the castle, "bom, bom, bom." The bridge rattled down, raising a cloud of dust as it struck the far edge of the moat. The gates went up with a creaking clatter of chains, and Mandor rode forth, Huld at his side, Dazzle just behind them. Before them floating in air, went Borold, stately, just at the level of the heads of the horses. "Oh, Borold," lamented Silkhands. "How silly. How silly you are."

From her place Silkhands could hear nothing of what went on between Mandor and the High King. She saw it all. She saw Huld salute the Demon of the High King, saw Dazzle summoned forward to bow and pose and talk and gesture. Even from that great distance the whole was unmistakable. She could even have put the words into their mouths, the suspicious whine of the High King, the assertion by Mandor that Windlow was not in Bannerwell, the testimony of Dazzle that the old man was in the Bright Demesne, that some of the culprits who had taken him were possibly even now on their way to challenge Bannerwell while another of them was probably hiding in the caves beneath the fortress. Smile, smile, pose, pose. The Demons frowned, spoke, spoke again.

At last the High King nodded his head, snarled something from one side of his mouth, and rode forward, some of his company behind him, though the greater part still covered the hills to the north. Silkhands saw Signalers flicking from place to place, saw the host to the east begin to scurry and shift to meet a new threat from that direction, finally saw the High King and his close attendants ride within Bannerwell's walls, and the great gate close behind him.

"Allies," Silkhands whispered to herself. "From challengers to allies, within the hour. Oh, Himaggery, I hope you know what it is you are doing."

Had she looked upward at that moment she would have seen an Elator poised above her on a stony prominence, watching the scene as she herself had done and with no less understanding. This was Himaggery's spy, gone to him in that instant to warn him of the unexpected alliance. But Silkhands fretted upon the mountain, thinking perhaps to come warn me, or trudge off through the forest looking for someone else to tell, or hope to intercept Himaggery, or perhaps just curl up in a ball where she was and pray that the world would not notice her until it had stopped its foolishness. As it was, she did none of these things. She simply sat where she was and waited to see what would happen. . . .

I, of course, knew none of this. I had gone from fury to martyred sulkiness, from rage to wounded sensitivity in the space of an hour or so. I had decided that Mavin was my mother and that I hated her, and then that she could not be my mother to have spoken to me as she had, and then that it didn't matter. I had cursed Mertyn, briefly, before remembering it was Mandor who had injured me, after which I cursed him. The echoing caverns accepted all this without making any response. Rage or sobs were all one to the cave. It amplified each equally and sent it back to me from a dozen directions in solemn mockery until I was tired of the whole thing. Even while all this emotion was going on, some cold part of my brain began to plan what I would do next and why and whether this or that option might be a good thing to consider. So, when I was done making insufferable noises for my own benefit, what needed to be done next was already there in my brain, ready to be accomplished.

Windlow had spoken of Ghost Pieces and Ghost Talents. It was apparent that the caves contained ghosts enough to make a great host, among them most of the Talents which would have been available in a sizeable Demesne. If Dorn could command such Talents, then I could do it as well. However, Ghosts alone might not be enough. The other Talents were there in the pouch at my belt, waiting to be taken. I could have taken Sorcerer, but did not. The mere holding of power would not suit my need. Seer? For what? What would happen would happen within hours, perhaps moments. There would be no need to See more than I might see with my eyes. Demon? Grimpt's small Talent in that direction seemed enough for the present circumstances. I had no useful thoughts about an Armiger's flight or a Sentinel's fire. No. Moved by some adolescent sense of the fitness of things, some desire to win at least some Game of my own, I chose to meet Mandor upon his own ground. I took into my left hand and clutched fast the tiny carved figure of Trandilar, First of the line of Queens and Kings and all lesser nobility.

It came upon me like the warmth of the sun, like the wooing of the wind, gentle, insistent, inexorable. She spoke to me in a voice of rolling stars, heavenly, a huge beneficence to hold smaller souls in thrall. She took me as a lover, as a child, as a beloved spouse, exhalted me. Adoration swept over me, then was incorporated within me so that it was I who was loved, the world one which loved me, followed me, adored me. All, all would follow me if I but used this beguilement upon them. Within was the sound of a chuckle, a satisfied breath, not the weary sigh of Dorn but a total satiety of love, love, love. "Trandilar," I said, speaking her name in homage and obeisance.

"Peter . . ." came the spirit voice in reply. Oh, surely Barish had done more than merely force a pattern onto some inanimate matter when he had made these Gamesmen. For the moment I could not move or think as myself. For that moment I was some halfway being, not myself, not Trandilar.

And then it passed, as Dorn had passed, leaving behind all the knowledge and Talent of that so ancient being. I had no fear, now, of Mandor's minions. Compared to this . . . this, his was a puny Talent, fit only for Fluglemen and Pigherders.

From that moment I was no longer a boy. Why should one raise up the dead and remain innocent, but raise up love and fear death? I leave that to you to figure out. I only learned in that moment that it was true.

So, I went back down the dusty corridors, following the prints which Silkhands and I had left toward the end of our journey, then relying upon memory and some instinct to guide me to that same cavern in which the dead kings had so recently been raised. Once there I did that thing which Dorn had taught me how to do, heard that spectral voice once more call into time, "Who comes, who comes, who comes . . ."

And answered it. "One who calls you forth, oh King, you and your forebears and your kin and your children, your followers and your minions, your Armigers, Sor-

cerers, Demons and Tragamors, your Sentinels and
Elators, come forth, come forth at my command; rise up
and do my will."

The King spoke to me, like a little chill wind in my
ear, softly crying, "Call thy Game, oh spirit. Call thy
Game and we will follow thee . . ."

14

Challenge and Game

The outflung ramparts of Malplace Mountain stretch far
from the summit to east and north, opening in one place
to permit the River Banner to loop around Bannerwell,
thrusting out both east and west of that fortress to push
the river north and, on the east, making a long ridge of
stone through which the river washed its way in time
long past. It cuts now through that ridge like a silver
knife, and the place is named the Cutting of Havajor
Dike, or often just "The Cut." From the eastern side of
this dike one may see the bannerets on the spires of
Bannerwell, but the whole of it and its surroundings
cannot be seen until the dike itself is mounted. So it was
that Himaggery saw it first from the top of the dike, saw
the assembled hosts inside and out of it, the moat and
river around it. What he saw was not unexpected. His
Elators had kept him advised of all, of the High King's
arrival, of the Game Call, the negotiations, the unexpected alliance. Thus when he had ridden to the top of
the dike and dismounted, he did not waste a moment in
open-mouthed staring. He knew well enough what it
would look like.

Some of those with him were not so sanguine. Indeed,
the host before them was mightier than any could recall
in memory. The tents of the High King's array spread
north and west like a mushroom plot fruiting after rain.
Between the dike and the Banner the level plain was

filled with smaller contingents grouped around their ovens, and the sound of axes still rang from the forested slopes of Malplace Mountain above the ferry barges moored upon the river. Mertyn stared. Even Windlow sat up in his wagon and looked at the horde, bemused. "If I had not Seen it already," he is reported to have said, "I would have been amazed."

Himaggery was busy with the last of the huge curved mirrors, setting it in place upon the dike, bracing it well with strong metal stanchions and setting men ready to hold it or prop it up if it were overthrown. "It must withstand Tragamor push," he told them. "Brace yourselves and be ready . . ."

" 'Ware, Himaggery," said a Demon, close at hand. "Herald comes . . ."

And it was Borold once again, Borold showing off for Dazzle who stood resplendent upon the tower top of Bannerwell, Borold in his pride, glowing with it. He cast a look over his shoulder as he floated up the dike toward Himaggery, one long look to see her standing there. Windlow thought that in that look was such love and uncritical adoration as a god might instill into a new creation. "Except, how boring at last," he thought. "To have one always, always adoring one. But, perhaps gods do not get bored . . ." (You may wonder how I knew what he thought, what he said, what happened. Never mind. Eventually, I knew everything that had happened to everyone. Eventually I knew too much.)

It was Borold who trumpeted the Challenge to Game, Borold who spoke not only for Mandor but for Prionde, as well. Turning his head slightly so that his words could be heard behind him on the fortress walls, he cried, "All within sound of my voice pay heed: I speak for Mandor of Bannerwell, most adored, most jealously guarded, and for the High King, Prionde, of the High Demesne, most puissant, most terrible. I speak for these two in alliance here assembled to call Great Game and make unanswerable Challenge upon Himaggery, styled Wizard, who has in treacherous fashion betrayed the hospitality shown his followers by the High King by stealing away one dependent, the Seer Windlow, and who has betrayed the good will of Mandor by sending into his Demesne a spy, the Healer Silkhands. For these reasons and others, more numerous than the leaves upon the trees, all reasons of ill faith and betrayal, treachery and all ungameliness, do my Lords cry Challenge upon this Himaggery and wait his move. We cry True Game!"

Borold awaited answer, at first imperiously, then impatiently, finally doubtfully. Himaggery had paid him no attention, but had gone on fiddling with the great mirror. It was some time before Himaggery looked up and gave a signal to an Elator near him. By this time Borold was casting little glances over his shoulder as though to get some signal from the castle. The Elator vanished. Himaggery signaled once more and a Herald rose lazily from the ground, walked to confront Borold. He did not rise in air. He merely stood there and made the far mountains ring with his words.

"Hear the words of Himaggery, Wizard of the Bright Demesne. The Wizard does not cry True Game. The Wizard cries Death, Pain, Horror, Mutilation, Wounds, Blood, Agony, Destruction. The Wizard calls all these and more. HE IS NOT PLAYING!"

And with that there came a great light and a smell of fire moving like a little sun, hurtling out of the east, spreading somewhat as it came, driving toward the great mirror where it stopped, coalesced and was taken up by a Sorcerer who stood there, ready. The Sorcerer turned and released the little sun once more. The quiet troop of Tragamors who had been crouched on the stone stiffened, twisted in unison, bent their heads toward Bannerwell, and sent the bolt of force against the walls of the fortress. Even as it burst there with a shattering impact and a sound of thunder, another little sun shot into the waiting mirror, was caught, was sent after the first, and yet again and again.

Mertyn whispered in awe. "Gamelords, what is it? How have you done this . . ."

To which Himaggery replied, "We have only done what could have been done at any time during the last thousand years. We have used Tragamors, working in teams, to Move the power from place to place. The mirrors are only to catch it, focus it, make it easier for the Sorcerers to pull it in without losing it . . ."

"Ahh," said Mertyn, almost sadly, watching the walls where the lightning bolts struck and struck again. Those walls trembled, melted powdered, fell to dust. All before them fell to dust. The Gamesmen before them blazed like tiny stars and were gone. The tents blossomed. died. "Where does it come from, this power?"

"From various places," Himaggery answered him, somewhat evasively.

"It is better not to know," whispered Windlow. "Better not to think of it. Better merely to make an end to Bannerwell's pride and Prionde's vainglory, then go. Go on to something better."

But the end was not to be so quick in coming. A struggle broke out near the great mirror. It tipped, moved, and one of the hurtling suns sped past to splash against the far mountain in a cloud of flowing dust. Elators had materialized near the mirror and were trying to overturn it. Among the struggling Gamesmen the forms of fustigars slashed with white fangs, slashed, ran, turned to slash again—Shapeshifters, come up the dike in the guise of beasts.

" 'Ware, Himaggery," cried the watching Demon, and thrust him aside as an arrow flashed from above. They looked up into the faces of Armigers who had come upon them from the wooded sides of the mountain. The Demon signaled. A hurtling ball of fire flew in from the east, was sloppily intercepted by two Sorcerers without benefit of the focusing mirror, was released again, and tossed upward by the Tragamor. The Armigers fell screaming from the sky like clots of ambient ash. Once more the mirror stood upright and the balls of fire struck at the walls of the fortress.

And those walls fell. Himaggery held up his hand, a drum sounded. Far back to the east the sound echoed, relayed back, and back, beyond hearing. The hurtling fires came no more. He waited, poised, watching intently to see what would happen to that great horde before him.

Through the rent in the castle wall the assembled Gamesmen poured out like water, those who could fly darting across the Banner, others leaping into the flood to be carried away to the north, struggling to come to the flat banks there and flee away across the plains. There was a struggle going on in the courtyard which could be seen from the dike: Gamesmen of Bannerwell fighting against those of the High Demesne, red plumes against purple, the red plumes overcoming the purple to release the chains and let the bridge fall. Then the red clad followers of the High King fled the fortress, out across the bridge and the grassy plain, toward the red tents which stood upon the northern heights, running toward them as though safety might be found under that fragile covering.

Himaggery gestured once more. Once more the bolts came into the mirror and were cast forward, this time onto those red tents which burned and were gone. The fleeing Gamesmen turned, milled about, some fleeing to the west, others making for the fringes of the forest, still others turning back to throw themselves into the waters of the Banner. It was not long before Himaggery's men could look down the Cut and see the bodies of those who had drowned in the attempt to swim the Banner, panoplied in sodden glory, dead.

"Prionde?" whispered Windlow. "Was he in that rout?"

"Who could tell, old friend," said Himaggery. "Should we withhold our fire to save one King?"

"No," said Windlow, weeping. "No. We agreed. It shall be as quick and sure as can be done. No long, drawn out Game to make the weaker hope and hope and refuse to surrender. No. Do it quickly, Himaggery."

He answered through clenched teeth. "I'm trying."

Once more the bombardment stopped and Himaggery watched to see what was happening below. There was no movement in the fortress. There were no watchers on the battlements.

"How long?" Himaggery asked.

Windlow answered him, "Soon. When I Saw it in my vision, the sun was just at that place in the sky. They will come forth soon. Wait. Destroy no more . . ."

So they waited. Mertyn asked what they waited for, and Himaggery answered, "For the fulfillment of a vision, King. Windlow has Seen this place, this time. Your thalan is up to something there. See. See that gateway within the wall of the Fortress!"

It was the gateway to the place of tombs, the ceremonial gateway to the Caves of Bannerwell. It opened within the walls of the fortress. It could be seen clearly through the shattered walls from the dike as the guardians of those tombs fled outward, fleeing in horror from something which pursued them. And behind those fleeing Guardsmen came a horde, an array, a Ghost Demesne pouring out of their graves and sepulchres, the catacombs giving up their dead, an army of dust, of dreams, of undying memory; battalions of bones, regiments of rags and rust, spear points red with corruption and time, swords eaten by age, bodies through which the wind moved, inspirited by shadow, tottering, clattering, moaning, sighing as the wind sighs, and calling as with one voice an ultimate horror, "We come, we come, we come . . . to take revenge upon the living, we who no longer live . . ."

They passed through the gateway, across the courtyard like moving shade, and through the great oaken doors of the castle, as though those doors were curtains of gauze. The Guardsmen who had stayed to guard the caves fled through the shattered walls of the fortress and into Himaggery's hands. An enemy held no terror for those who had seen the dead march. I came behind them. They could not be led, only sent, so I had sent them into the castle and stood waiting for them in the castle yard. They would return again, but they would not return alone. I had commanded it.

I felt the eyes of Himaggery's men on my back. Though I did not turn, I knew well they were there. I had seen them when the gates flew open, had seen the great rent in the fortress wall, knew that others Moved even as I Moved, that all came to a point at this hour. I waited, calm now. Time was done for any foolish blathering. There were no questions now. Only answers, at last.

Then it happened. The doors to the castle burst wide, and the followers of Mandor fled forth, white and trembling, falling, crawling, vomiting on the stones, clutching their way across those slimed stones like crippled creatures, crabwise slithering away, away from what came behind. I saw Dazzle, and Huld, and a hundred faces I had seen in Mandor's halls, the High King, and followers of his. They came forth in a flood and saw me, and seeing me they knelt down or fell down before me and cried to me for help. "King," "Prince," they cried, bending their knees to me, leaning upon their hands and beating their foreheads upon the stone.

And I told them to be still and wait. Be still, I said, for Mandor comes.

As at last he did. No less white than they, no less horrified, and yet with some dignity yet and a pathetic attempt at beguilement. Even now, even now he tried to use Talent upon *me* and still he wound it about himself.

I motioned him to kneel. I said, "I have shown you your dead, Mandor. I have brought you your dead. The ancient ones you have dishonored. The newly dead you have robbed of life. Some among them have Game to call against you, so they tell me . . ."

If it were possible for him to grow more pale, he did so. I looked from him to Dazzle. "And there are other dead, Dazzle. Your mother, I think, and others perhaps. Would you have them brought here to join those we have brought from the Caves of Bannerwell?"

She did not answer me. I had not thought she would. She was too busy clutching the power to herself, weaving, weaving as Mandor was. Well, Let them weave. The Ghost army crowded out of the castle door, moving toward these pitiful mortals, moving to trample them, take them up, inhabit them, clothe themselves in life again . . . Dorn within me cautioned me. Before they grew stronger, it was time to send them back . . . back . . .

And then, of a sudden, if was as though someone lifted a great heaviness from me. Before me the Ghosts began to waver. They cried softly, once, twice, and were gone. A sound swept through my head like wind in pines and the smell of rain. Dazzle looked up at me, horrid that face. Mandor saw her, screamed, and screamed again as his people looked upon him and scrawled away from him, away and away, clutching at one another like survivors of some great flood, and casting glances backwards at him in horror. Then it was that Mandor and Dazzle flew at one another, clawing, striking with their hands, locked in a battle of ultimate despair.

Behind me someone spoke my name. "Peter. Enough. We have come to Bannerwell as you have asked."

I turned. It was that lean man, Riddle, the Immutable, the leader of the Immutables, Tossa's father.

"I have been told what you tried to do," he said. "For Tossa. I thank you."

"It was useless," I wept. "Useless, as this has been. But I tried to . . ."

"I know," he touched my arm. Then I saw others behind him, Chance, Yarrel.

"You got there," I said stupidly. "You got back."

Yarrel's eyes were on Mandor and Dazzle, not upon me. His expression was one I dreaded, full of horror and contempt. I knew what he was thinking and did not want him to say it, but he did. "See there," he whispered. "This is what Talents do. This is all that they do, and I have had enough of it . . ."

"Shhh," said Riddle. "We have agreed. Part of the blame is ours. We have allowed it to go on. And we are agreed that it must end . . ."

"While you are here, they cannot use their *Talents,*" he spit the word at me. "But when you are gone, Riddle, they will use them once more. And again. And again." He turned away and went through the shattered wall, his shoulders heaving. Once he turned to look back and saw my face, saw something there, perhaps, which moved him for a moment. His hand moved as though he would have gestured to me in friendship, but his face hardened in that moment and he turned away.

I knew what I could do. I could follow him. Soon we would be away from Riddle's force or power or Talent and my own would be useable once more. Then I could evoke Trandilar, and Yarrel would love me as once he had done—more, more. He would adore me. As

Mandor's people had done. Oh, for the moment I
wanted that. Yes. For that moment I wanted that.

And then I did not want that at all, never, not Yarrel.
I miss him. I have not seen him, but I know he is well.
Some days I need him greatly, greatly, more than I can
say. Perhaps, Someday . . . well. All time is full of
somedays.

After a long time full of many confusions, we came
away from Bannerwell. Dazzle and Mandor stayed behind, together with Huld and a few others—and the Immutables. Neither of them can hide what they are any
longer. They are what they are.

I imagine them there, inhabiting the corridors and
stairways of Bannerwell, drifting like shadows down
long, silent staircases, vanishing behind hangings, seen
at a distance upon a crenellated battlement, dark shadows, moving blots, heard in the long nights as the wind is
heard, a ceaseless moan, never encountering one another except to see a shade vanish from a lighted room, to
hear a cry down a chimney stack from some long unused
place within that mountain of stone which is Bannerwell.

I imagine them awake in the dark hours, veiled by
night, hidden in gloom, plodding endless aisles of opu-
lent dust in the Caves of Bannerwell to look upon the
tombs, to dream of such a silence, such a healing as that,
for on the tombs the marble dead sleep whole and
unblemished, softly gleaming in torchlight, forever safe
except to one such as I—such as I.

I think of Huld, hopeless and without honor, committed to his endless servitude, his mordacious kinship
with horror, and I imagine that he follows them there,
down those endless halls, watering the sterile dust with
his tears.

Will we meet again, Mandor and I? I do not think he

will live long. I would not if I were he.

But—I am not he.

And I—I returned with Himaggery to the Bright Demesne. We found Silkhands upon the mountain and
brought her with us. She was changed by it all. She does
not talk as much now as she used to. But then, neither
do I.

Windlow is here with us. Riddle comes to meet with
Himaggery now and again. Our part of the world is only
a small part of the world. Elsewhere there are Guardians and Councils and Wizardly doings and much perse-
cution of Heresy. There are plans afoot. When a little
time has passed, I may have heart to take part in them.

Just now I do not take part in much. Himaggery says
he is sure there is a way Talents such as mine can be
fitted into a world which Yarrel would approve, a way in
which a Peter and a Yarrel may continue to be friends.
Just now, however, that world seems far away and long
into the future.

So, I think on that and 'imagine' what such a world
might be like. What might my place in it be? I am such
an animal as they have not known before, a Shifter-
King-Necromancer who may, if he chooses, become
Sorcerer, Seer, Sentinel—and every other thing as well.
I must leave here to decide about that, I think. I must
find Mavin. I think she knows something which all these
solemn men have not yet thought of.

The fruit trees bloom in the mists of the Bright Demesne. Soon will be Festival time. I shall no longer sew
ribbons upon my tunic to run the streets as a boy. King's
blood one. King's blood ten. King's blood, and the
world waits.